KERRY CURSON

Anwen and the Island

First published by Little Grebe Books 2023

This novel is entirely a work of fiction. The names, characters and incidents portrayed in it are the work of the author's imagination. Any resemblance to actual persons, living or dead, events or localities is entirely coincidental.

First edition

ISBN: 978-1-3999-6370-1

Cover art by Winona Kieslich

This book was professionally typeset on Reedsy.
Find out more at reedsy.com

For my fellow daydreamers...

Acknowledgement

Thank you to Jon, Jan, Olivia and Freddie, you were the only people to know that all this writing was quietly going on. Thank you for reading my words and never doubting me for a moment.

Thank you to editor Roisin Heycock for being the first reader of the full manuscript of *Anwen and the Island,* and for giving me some wonderful advice on making Anwen's world come to life.

A special thanks to the cover artist Winona Kieslich who gladly made many small tweaks to get my vision just as I wanted it, and to all of the people that supported the crowdfunder that got this book to the printers and into bookshops across Wales and beyond.

Lastly, thanks to Little Grebe Books, a collective creation of passionate authors supporting and mentoring more writers into publication.

1

Chapter 1

For a time, my life was perfect. I didn't know it then. Because when perfect is all you've ever known, you have nothing else to compare it to. My father was a celestial cartographer and a sailor. The first title means he made maps of the stars. Mostly to help other sailors and explorers navigate their way around the world. Once, the King of Hetu Island described my father's job as 'mapping the heavens' which sounds way better than 'celestial cartographer' - to me anyway.

The second title means that we got to live on a sailboat, for being a sailor is necessary when you want to travel the world at the drop of a hat- or a pilot – but we are seafarers. If you have never seen a sailboat before, let me tell you, it's the best home a kid could want. It looks sort of like a pirate ship – but less scary. There are huge masts with sails that look like giant kites, they also double up as the tallest kind of climbing frame. Dad named our boat Shelagh after his late mother. When I had asked Dad why he'd decided Shelagh was a girl boat he simply answered:

"Look how strong and magnificent she is. No man could

be as fierce as Shelagh." That's why I loved him so much – he made me feel like I could do anything.

I was born in 1918. The day I arrived into the world was just two weeks after World War 1 was over. Phew. Our boat had an engine too, but mostly, Mum and Dad rode on the winds. Until they didn't.

Living out at sea meant that my home was the sky, a direct line into infinity. I think the sky is the wisest thing to ever exist. It has watched the world for hundreds and thousands of years. I didn't often meet other children back then, but when the grownups described the sky as blue, I'd have to bite my tongue not to argue. Because the sky is technicolour, depending on where you watch from. My favourite kind of sunsets are those painted in wisps of pink and purple. It's like being inside a painting. My garden was the ocean, deep, playful and brooding. Mum's main role was taking care of me, but she was also far nimbler than my Dad. She could shinny up the masts to fix, or unfix rope, faster than anyone I'd ever known. Her legs were long and muscular. She was like a mermaid chimp; an incredible climber with wild blonde hair always whipping up around her face. She seemed happy to me. Now I understand that she wasn't. Living at sea can be lonely for a grown up. I loved every moment.

The salty air lived within my every cell. It lived on my chapped but happy lips. I could never get rid of the taste of salt. Salt slept within the strands of my long, unkempt hair, making it feel more like dried seaweed. Each morning I would wake myself up by diving into the warm and salty embrace of the Chaleurian Sea. This is where we spent the years that I can remember. Dad would plan our travel around the storms. Down inside my ocean garden, the rainbow-colored coral would wave and dance 'Good morning' to me each day. Hundreds of other creatures large and small, from clownfish to manta ray were my friends. Mum always said there was never a time I couldn't swim. Each day I would try to hold my breath for just a little longer in hope that I could one day live as a mermaid. I would count the seconds in my head and then write my records down in my notebook.

"Dad! I got to three minutes!" I shouted out with joy as I burst up through the water's glassy surface.

"Well done my little mermaid." Nothing made my heart sing more than my Dad's proud smile.

By night, I was lulled to sleep by the gentle rocking of our sailboat, Shelagh. A cacophony of stars rolling into forever were my nightlights. Their stories swam into my mind and heart upon my Dad's velvet smooth voice. My favourite thing for Dad to read to me was a poem called 'If' by Rudyard Kipling. It was written for a son, but Dad changed the end so that it was especially for me:

If you can keep your head when all about you
Are losing theirs and blaming it on you,
If you can trust yourself when all men doubt you,
But make allowance for their doubting too;
If you can wait and not be tired by waiting,
Or being lied about, don't deal in lies,
Or being hated, don't give way to hating,
And yet don't look too good, nor talk too wise:

If you can dream—and not make dreams your master;
If you can think—and not make thoughts your aim;
If you can meet with Triumph and Disaster
And treat those two impostors just the same;
If you can bear to hear the truth you've spoken
Twisted by knaves to make a trap for fools,
Or watch the things you gave your life to, broken,
And stoop and build 'em up with worn-out tools:

If you can make one heap of all your winnings
And risk it on one turn of pitch-and-toss,
And lose, and start again at your beginnings
And never breathe a word about your loss;
If you can force your heart and nerve and sinew
To serve your turn long after they are gone,
And so hold on when there is nothing in you

Except the Will which says to them: 'Hold on!'

If you can talk with crowds and keep your virtue,
Or walk with Kings—nor lose the common touch,
If neither foes nor loving friends can hurt you,
If all men count with you, but none too much;
If you can fill the unforgiving minute
With sixty seconds' worth of distance run,
Yours is the Earth and everything that's in it,
And—which is more—you'll be a Queen my love!

Looking back, it seems like our life then might have been a dream. Dad's face is blurred in my mind now. But I remember his beard vividly. He had a deep brown beard that was tidy and groomed no matter what.

"Just because we live wild, doesn't mean we have to look it." He would say when I'd stand watching him shave each day, covering his face in white foam. That was his military voice. Navy. Not many people knew how to draw and compile maps of the stars back then. So, important people all over the world would seek out my dad to help them learn. My dad learned from his dad, who learned from his dad and so on. My great, great, great grandfather was born in Nuku Hiva, a Polynesian island. My dad was born in Wales – that adventure is a story I never got to hear. Because my perfect life changed forever when I was eleven years old.

"Laura, Anwen get up here quickly!" It was unlike Dad to sound so panicked.

"What? What is it?" Below deck was our living room, a bit more like a proper house. Mum scrambled up the wooden stairs to top deck. I followed using hands and knees like a lion – which I liked to do.

"There's a storm coming. We need to fire up the engines now." Mum turned to come back down.

"Anwen quick go back down."

"I want to see," I begged

"Anwen darling let me past then. Hurry up." Mum went quickly back below deck while I joined Dad who was stood looking outward to the horizon.

"What is it, Dad?" I followed his gaze, his forehead was furrowed making deep lines dance across it.

"I've never seen anything like it, storm season is still three months off." I don't think he was saying this to me, because he looked like he was in some strange trance. His face frozen, looking beyond our world. There was clear blue sky immediately above our head, but just a mile or so South, thick black clouds rolled and billowed. They were coming straight for us. Shelagh started to rock. The sea looked flat, but somehow tipped us playfully up and down.

"It's moving fast Anwen. Come on, downstairs."

Within a few tiny moments, the sea's playful rocking turned to deep anger. She now threw us from side to side. The force was so great, I thought we would capsize. Cracks of lightning ripped through the sky. I would have stayed and watched if it wasn't for Mum's terrified tug on my arm. She scooped me up and scrambled down the winding staircase to below deck. Dad's heavy footsteps drummed behind us, the butterflies painted on the walls blurred and made me dizzy. Mum's nails dug hard into my leg, as my weight got too much.

Below deck everything was bolted down tight, Mum pushed us into my small bedroom and Dad followed. My room was positioned at the centre of the boat, making it less likely to feel so under attack from the angry sea. Even my snow globe was screwed down to the surface of my bedside table. The snow globe world looked perfectly calm among our ensuing chaos, so I stared hard at it trying not to let my rising fear swallow me whole. Shelagh's rocking threatened to topple us over completely. We huddled together on my bedroom's tiny floor space. The only things un-anchored were my teddies. In one blow they flew upward, landing down onto our huddle as a wave smashed our home down onto the water's surface. I still struggle to understand how something so fluid and tranquil can become so hard and destructive. Worried for my toy's safety, I tried to wriggle out of Mum and Dad's tight embrace.

"Anwen, no."

"But Mum–"

"-They're fine. Stay put."

If I'd have known this would be the last time in my bedroom. I would have pulled my patchwork quilt down onto the floor with us, and never let it go. I would have swept all my books out from the boxes under my bed and never let them go. My books were my magic. My other worlds. But I didn't know. So, I no longer have any of those things.

2

Chapter 2

The winds and tides pushed us North to a place I now know as Sedna Island. Our engines went down just as the storm receded, so we were aimlessly drifting along with the ocean's new found calm.

"The sea is just like you as a baby Anwen, post tantrum, when you'd get all tired and lay looking at the sky, a soft smile at your lips." Mum smiled in jest as she pinched at my cheek. The warm balmy air I was used to, had become a new world filled with cold, frosty mists. I stood at Shelagh's bow, leaning up over the rails trying to be the first to see what was up ahead.

"There's land Anwen." Dad called from the boom of the main sail.

"Really?" I could barely see anything through the thick mist that curtained the entire world in front of us.

"Laura, hold the sails, would you?" He asked, before disappearing below deck. Mum took his place, Dad returned seconds later with the his giant Atlas his eyes wide like a madman.

"Based on our position against Orion last night, we shouldn't see land for days." The giant book filled the whole of Dad's left arm. He licked at his index finger and thumb of his free hand and frantically flipped the pages of the book back and forth.

"This is an island, and it isn't on any map." He continued to flit through the pages, back and forth, back and forth just to be sure. I looked from him back into the mist. I too could now see the shadow of land just beyond us. Dad carelessly thrust his atlas to the bench.

"Girls we've discovered new land." He laughed, excited held Mum's childlike face in his hands planting a dramatic kiss on her lips and then he ran to me.

"Anwen my darling. We have discovered a new world. We will change this Atlas forever." He picked me up as though I was still five years old, and spun me around. I giggled with glee, so infectious was Dad's joy. Just as my feet touched back down upon Shelagh's deck we all jolted forward. Shelagh had found the seabed. The mist seemed to lift all of a sudden, or perhaps we had simply passed through it. The midnight blue of deep ocean had turned to the emerald green of shallower waters.

Seeing the island like that for the first time gave me the strangest feeling. My tummy lurched. Maybe my blood knew that something dark lived within the threads of this land. As Shelagh's belly began to slide more softly into sand banks, Dad dropped the anchors while Mum rummaged through the under seat storage boxes for warm clothes. She found me a woolen fleece which just about fit, and a hat she had knitted when she was a girl- which was a little too big- but it was green so I loved it all the same. Mum wore Dad's large yellow Macintosh coat as it lay at the top of the pile. All three of us had the same yellow coat, we just hadn't needed to wear them for a long time. Mum had lined all three with wool herself. Each winter item rolled neat and tight in their dedicated boxes, draws or cupboards.

Everything on the boat was about being tucked away or pinned down. I loved all of our secret compartments. Dad put on waders and lifted Mum to shore first, then me. The beach had a greyness to it. It's colours somehow muted.

I had never known a cold like it. Each breath puffed into the air like smoke, rising to heaven. Mum and Dad's noses went red at the tip making them look like little elves. Mum and I had wellies. Curious, I went running up the shingle beach towards a line of dense green trees; silver birch peppered among tall, graceful pines like ghosts.

"Anwen, don't run into the unknown so mindlessly. You will lose your way if you don't take care." I shrugged and lagged back to Mum and Dad's slower walking pace. The line of trees created a fortress to whatever lay beyond. We walked the perimeter twice before noticing a small window between the thicket. It opened out to form a narrow path. It had clearly been forged by humans as the neighbouring branches were cut clean. Not snapped. Dad walked up front, I was in the middle with Mum behind. Birds cawed from above. Maybe they were telling us to go back.

After a mile or so we reached a wide open clearing. Nine small thatched cottages were all set out in a semi-circle around the edge of trees. Each was identical to the next, with walls made of stone, doors made of a dark wood. The windows were framed openings made with the same dark wood as the doors. Hey made up the beautiful patterns of their rooftops, and each had a small front garden with snowdrops and plastic covered sheds abundant with growing vegetables. Each roof had a chimney that smoked. It was a mirrored land. In the centre of the semi-circle was a large pentagon shaped building with a wood carving of a serpent and a bird above its threshold. The roof of this huge building spiralled higher than the treetops and seemingly as wide. The diameter could have fit five of those small cottages inside, it towered above everything else. I felt so small against it all.

Usually when we arrived at new places there was someone expecting us, or busy town folk working the sea shores ready to greet visitors that brought them trade and stories of adventure. This place seemed sleepy and abandoned. It felt intrusive wandering around without welcome or guide. Dad walked up the path of the first house while Mum and I waited beyond the path. A woman answered wearing a black dress and white apron, with a white matching hat. Dad spoke to her a moment, I couldn't hear what he said. The woman looked passed him at Mum and I as he talked. She then stood back and opened the door in invitation for all three of us to enter. Inside, the room was dark but warmed by a large open fireplace. A wooden table sat in the centre of the room with four chairs around it. She invited us to sit. The smell of garlic simmering slowly in the saucepan made me feel a little more at home.

The woman's behaviour was welcoming in all the ways a person might describe a warm welcome. She smiled a lot, talked briskly about the weather and offered for us to eat with her, but there was something cold and lifeless about her. Her eyes lacked emotion. Her smile stayed frozen at her mouth. It didn't crease and sweeten her eyes like it did on all other faces. Her hair was tied back into a tight ponytail under her hat. It made her round face harsher still. She invited Mum and Dad to sit at the kitchen table.

"I have a son, Justin. He stays in the parlour room. Would you like to meet him? He's eleven, similar to you I expect?" She bent over resting her hands on her knees to make herself my height. Adults never usually did this to me. It made me aware of how small I was.

"That's right, Anwen is eleven too." Dad broke the silence for me.

"I'd like to stay here please." The thought of leaving Mum and Dad unnerved me. In the darkness of the room shadows fell across the woman's face.

"It will be fine. Children belong together. Don't you think?" The woman countered, smiling again.

"I'd prefer she stay here right now." I restated and then Dad added

"We've had a challenging few days." The woman smiled at his answer and backed off.

"I'm Camille by the way." Camille shook Mum's hand first, and then Dad's but she didn't offer it to me as most adults did.

"Laura." Mum smiled.

"Guy." My dad nodded, but he kept his facial expression blank. He always did this when meeting new people. He remained unreadable, until he had his summation of them. I sat on Dad's lap. The wooden table was old and unvarnished. Knife scratches from chopping food crossed its surface. I stroked my finger over them.

"Would you like a mug of warm milk?"

"Yes, please." The three of us echoed in sync and laughed. Camille's eyes flashed to me, and she did that false smile that didn't meet her eyes again. She turned and busied herself pouring milk into a saucepan and placing it on the stove.

"It's been a cold two days out there." Dad told the woman of how we had been blown completely off course. She stood and listened intently.

"The sea is a dangerous place." She commented at last.

"Our people do not venture beyond this shore, and we are wary of visitors." She served Mum and Dad their milk and then placed a cup of steaming water in front of me.

"Oh I wanted milk." I corrected. Dad squeezed my arm in quiet reprimand.

"Children don't drink milk with the adults here. It's a scarce commodity. You all have energy enough, don't you think?" She pinched softly at my cheek attempting endearment, it was too soon to assume my immaturity. I didn't like it.

Dad whispered to me,

"We must respect any local customs here. Okay?" I stayed silent. Mum spoke up next.

"I'm sorry. Anwen usually lives on a level playing field with us. Our life together is unique. She is used to her freedoms, but she likes water to drink too, don't you Anwen?" I nodded. This felt strange. I sensed an oddity about it all. Camille then offered honey to sweeten the milk, both Mum and Dad accepted. I could smell the sweetness of it. It was both comforting and annoying because I was so hungry.

"Is there somewhere we might stay a few days while I make some repairs to our boat? It's not too big a task- some torn sails and a damaged engine. I have the parts I need." His voice broke a silence filled with sharp edges.

"We have a governor of the island. He teaches daily sermons. I can talk to him this afternoon. He's my cousin. We are usually wary of strangers. This island was once a place of great savagery. My cousin has really turned things around." She smiled then, the first real smile that creased the corners of her eyes, eyes that seemed to drift off to another place when she spoke of her cousin. Her face was blissful then. She looked almost pretty as the sunlight shone through the kitchen window and lit her face. She was basking in whatever memory she had awoken in speaking of her cousin – the governor. She was brought back into the room by Dad coughing, she continued

"Of course I can feel that you are good people. What a treacherous way to live life on a sailboat though. I must say." Camille sat down at the table to share in the adult milk drinking ritual.

"The storm was quite terrifying." Mum agreed, her brow furrowed as she recalled it all.

"It was certainly a surprise-" Dad interjected, ready to make light of a tough encounter as he always did

"-But our way of life is exciting. To live at one with the elements…it's certainly not easy, but I wouldn't have it any other way. Would you?"

He looked to Mum then, she was taking a sip of her drink so she just shook her head 'no'.

"Well I'm sure we share the custom of keeping our children safe." Camille commented as she placed her hand on top of Mum's which was absently resting on the table top. Their eyes met and Mum smiled weakly.

"Always." Mum whispered, her own eyes glazed into a stare off into some distant thought.

3

Chapter 3

Obeah was the governor. He was a large, broad-shouldered man with a broad smile and a laugh that rumbled out into the room like the tremors of an earthquake. It couldn't go unnoticed. As the whole town gathered within that giant pentagon building known as the *congregational space,* my little family suddenly stood out like a peacock at a crow's house. Everyone dressed in black and white except for us. I still wore my faded red dress underneath a blue woollen jumper Mum had found earlier that day. This was paired now with my yellow rain Mac. Dad was in a rusty orange knit jumper and shorts having finally removed his waders. Mum was in a green dress and tights under her own yellow coat. All the other towns people were either in black trousers, white shirt, or black dresses, even the children- except Obeah. He wore a white linen shirt and trousers with a red silk scarf tied at his neck. The scarf was printed in hundreds of little golden flowers. It was a small thing, but it made me think of kings and queens.

This room reminded me of the church where Mum's brother

got married when I was six. We sailed from Jamala to Nicaragua to make it there. They married in a small church, more like a hut apart from the large cross on the roof and the crosses on every wall inside.

This place was also like a hut in its feel. It was a wooden building with five external walls and no others inside to break it into rooms. The space was completely open. Large windows on each wall and one large glass slice in the pitched ceiling, made it bright with sunlight, which I loved. Chairs filled half of the room, all facing a lectern. Behind the lectern, a large tree trunk, a silver birch, poured out from the floor and through the roof where it disappeared. I realised later that this acted as a flagpole which explained the levers and pulleys drilled into its side – it was the winch system that would raise the flag every sermon, and leave it there until sunset each day. Stood outside later I would see the branches were stripped, leaving behind only the trunk and a white flag. The flag had a coiled snake with a bird of prey stood upon it painted in black, the same as the carvings above the entrance to the building. Inside the congregational space, and behind the silver birch flagpole the entire wall was painted in a mural – a scene of nature. It was an image of a forest, with a winding river that was home to a giant snake like water creature. The picture showed two halves of the sky; part day, part night. The first half a sunset filled with fiery crimson and warm yellows. I already missed the warmth of the Chaudarian sun so much. The other half of the image showed the stars sat side by side like brothers and sisters of the sky. Seeing this for the first time gave me a strange sense of longing. A yearning feeling like the mild pain I get in my belly when I miss someone. Although I didn't know who or what I was aching for. There was no reason for me to detect my family splintering yet.

The adults were all trying to push in towards Obeah as he spoke to people in turn. It was like he had his own gravitational pull and anyone that came close to him got sucked into his orbit. Mum and Dad finally got through the crowd to introduce themselves to him. I'd found a spot in the corner of the room to quietly watch it all unfold. They shook hands and chatted, Mum smiled so brightly as they talked and laughed. I hadn't seen her smile like that in a long time. It made me smile too, and a little worry melted away. It seemed as though the whole island was here, maybe fifty people all together- only fifteen of these were children. They all sat in a quiet circle in the opposite corner to me reading the same books as one another, mirrored like the cottages and the clothes. Strange. I usually liked to make friends, but I didn't want to break into the reading circle. I missed my books – it was a good way to hide, burying your head in a book. Grown-ups are always happy to see kids sat quietly reading. Reading is clever, they think. What kids know is that reading is magic.

Obeah walked right by me, leading Mum and Dad to the front of the room.

"You are welcome upon our island as long as you need. Our community is about dedication to kindness and the greater good. If you will share in that sense of hope and transcendence, you will always have a warm home and a family in us." He placed his hand on the small of my mother's back and their eyes met locking into place. Obeah and my Dad began talking then, they were of similar stature; broad and in need of ducking through the average doorway. Obeah smiled broadly at my mother, just like Camille had when welcoming us into her home. Like Camille's, his smile didn't quite reach beyond the apples of his cheeks. His eyes were still and blank as glass. Obeah and Dad were then interrupted by a boy with white hair and grey blue eyes. The boy whispered something to Obeah, who nodded, then the boy quickly left. He had not been part of the circle of children sat reading. Obeah and Dad chatted quietly, I couldn't hear a thing. But I could see plenty. My dad was a man that had walked in the presence of kings and given speeches to some of the most important people in the world. He always did these things with a proud chest, relaxed shoulders and unfaltering confidence. I could see with Obeah, there was something uneasy in the way Dad stood. He fidgeted his hands in and out of his pockets, rested them by his side and put them back again. His weight rocked from foot to foot, unsteady, until Obeah moved on to talk with someone else. Obeah had something to say to everyone, and circled the room to ensure he gave time to each member of the community, but the person who took most of his attention, was my mum. His eyes wandered to her often, and when he was anywhere near her he would throw a comment her way and she would laugh or nod in agreement.

Then a loud crash. The high pitched, brain rattling sound of metal clanging and glass smashing. At that moment, everyone in the room turned to look in the direction of the offending sound. I had seen the whole thing unfold just before, as if in slow motion; A strong built red haired girl had entered through the double doors. Smiling, she was a burst of colour and joy with her bouncy red curls and rosy cheeks. She'd come through the doors backwards, pushing her back against them, while her hands were occupied by a large silver tray filled with drinks. As she had turned to face the room, proud of her manoeuvre, she tripped on the entrance rug. The silver tray and all of its glass contents smashed to the floor. The red haired girl looked up from her hands and knees, stunned by the noise herself.

"I'm so sorry." She whimpered before running straight back out again. The whole room remained frozen to the spot, staring at the discarded mess. Obeah's face iced over, it was so quick it could have been a flash of lightening. He resumed his wooden smile and continued talking quietly again to the boy with white hair and grey-blue eyes who had quietly returned to his side. The boy left the hall through the double doors without a second glance at the mess on the floor. A tall, clumsy looking boy scrambled apologetically from the group of reading children, his hair was black making him look pale, especially with his accompanying black jumper and trousers. He scurried to the mess on the floor, lowering to his knees, he began scooping up the mess. I couldn't watch on and do nothing like everyone else, so I jumped up to help. Carefully we picked at the large chunks of glass before the boy pulled out a handkerchief and swept the smaller crystals into a pile.

"They're the most harmful pieces, though they're small." He whispered while signing with his hands, the handkerchief sat in a mound atop the collected crumbs on the floor.

"I know, I once had a tiny glass splinter in my foot and could barely walk for days. I squeezed it out myself in the end." I felt proud of that bit of the story, of my ability to take the pain of that horrible splinter.

The room resumed itself around us; the adults restarted their chatter and began making their way to their seats. The boy scrunched the last of the mess into his handkerchief and placed it on the tray.

"Thank you." He mouthed with exaggerated movements of his lips, his hands moving in sync with his words like before. He tapped his palm to his chin and then gestured his hand towards me. He was saying 'thank you' in sign language. I recognised it from a performance I had once watched when visiting the island of Nelawi with Mum and Dad. The boy picked up the tray and left through the double doors. I followed him.

Outside, he looked around him for where to go with his tray. Both of us looked to the right as we heard the sobs of the red haired girl coming from among the trees that surrounded the central village. The tall boy walked towards her, and again, I followed. He placed the tray down on a tree stump and knelt in front of the girl.

"Are you okay Egret?" He was talking with his voice and his hands again, his dark hair covered his face now as he leant forward. He swept it back and tucked a strand behind his ear.

"Course not. Everyone saw…Justin came looking for me. That's why I'm hiding." She sniffed "I'm supposed to be raising the flag during the sermon today. Obeah will think me unworthy…like everyone always does."

"Not true." The boy spoke and gestured with his hands. The red haired girl, Egret, wiped her face on the sleeve of her black dress and looked up at me.

"Who are you?" She asked.

"I'm Anwen. My family and I arrived today. We were sort of pushed here by the recent storm. I think we're staying while my dad fixes our boat."

"You've picked a strange time to come…" she trailed off.

"Well that's okay. We've been to some unusual places. We'll leave in a few days. What are your names?" I tried to make sure the boy could see my lips assuming he couldn't hear me.

"Thomas." Said the boy.

"Egret." Said the girl. Egret stood and smoothed the front of her dress brushing away the dust from the ground behind her. She continued-

"Come on we best get back in there. Sermon is starting. Obeah will want an extra strong display if we have visitors."

I followed Thomas and Egret back inside the congregational space. Everyone now sat down, Obeah at the lectern. The room fell to immediate silence. I quietly joined Mum and Dad near the front row of seats. Obeah said nothing at first, he simply spread his arms wide as if he were opening up for a hug. I looked over my shoulder, all eyes were fixed on Obeah. His loud bellowing voice, the bass guitar of this merry performance began to preach.

"An auspicious day islanders, for the winds have pushed some guests our way. Please join me in welcoming Laura, Guy and Anwen McQueen to Sedna island." Everyone stood from their seats and clapped until Obeah swiped his hands like a conductor quieting his orchestra, like robots the room stopped clapping and sat back down.

"*The Sky Ones,* our Gods beyond the stars must be pleased with this year's toil to have sent us such a symbol of thanks – new friends. I feel more rewards are coming our way. The rewards for all of labour, keep working my good people. Vexed Goddess Kunda will threaten us no more." The room chorused a hum of agreement. It all got more and more boring from there- sea serpents and bird warriors were waiting to punish people for such silly things; Dancing, Singing... you name it, if it was fun, it was ruled out. I stopped listening, letting his words blur and dance undetected upon my ear drum. I watched Mum the whole time, she was completely mesmerized. I wanted to laugh. It actually rose into my throat, that big burst from my tummy when I was about to get the giggles- but I held it tight inside my mouth. My head felt like it would burst. She looked down at me still smiling and nudged me with her elbow. I liked her like this.

A few oddities seeped into my mind as the governor went on and on

"…appeasing *Kunda* monster of the sea…..." I picked at a loose piece of rubber on the leg of my wellington boot, his words droned on "…a life made eternal and safe…..dedicated to a loving leader……sacrifice for love…dedicated to the *Sky Ones*."

4

Chapter 4

A few days had turned into a week. We were staying in a small out house behind Obeah's grand lodge. His was the largest home on the whole island, set back from the rest of the community atop a hill that was enclosed within oak, and sycamore trees. The children of the island were schooled in the congregation space each day. As we were just guests, I was not a part of this. So, our days were our own for a while longer. Dad left early each morning to work on Shelagh, Mum seemed happy to help Obeah in his vast garden that was filled with a rainbow of Camelia and Gorse, flowers that could still hold steadfast to the cold of this place. I was free to take to the forest.

I discovered very quickly that the whole island was only a few miles in diameter, which meant I could explore the entire place from one side to the other in a few days. The trees here were less spiky than on warmer islands we had visited in the past. It made them seem kinder in some ways, but they were so much more difficult to climb. Their bark was darker from being wet all the time, but tougher when dry. Climbing an oak tree was more challenging than climbing a palm tree because the gaps in the bark were so much narrower, and if you hit a wet, soft area you were done for. Although, a misstep on a palm would easily rip through the thin skin of a shin, so 'six of one, half a dozen of the other' as Dad would often say. The branches of oak trees were more solid though. This meant I could easily climb up high and just sit for a couple of hours watching the world below.

It was during this first exploration that I discovered a nest of nuthatches. Tiny little tree climbing birds with dusky, ocean blue-black wings, and a sunset orange breast. The little family were all huddled together cosily in a knot of the great oak's belly. On spotting me perched on the branch, the tiniest one panicked and began to wriggle. Their tweets all rang out in chorus, as if trying to reassure their baby sibling not to do anything rash. The poor thing. I realised in that moment that it was right to be afraid of me. I was a giant to them, a giant with the ability to crush the whole little family with one thump of my fist. Not that I ever would. Never. The runt bird got into such a fluster that it toppled right out of the nest, landing into a bed of leaves on the ground. There was no parent bird in sight.

"Oh you silly thing, trying to run all alone. Come here." I swung downward from the branch and let go, dropping the few feet to the floor.

"It's okay tiny baby, I won't hurt you, I promise." Conscious not to get my scent on the bird in fear its mother would reject it, I gathered a pile of leaves in both hands and scooped the frightened bird into them.

"It will be okay, I promise." I looked around realising that I now needed to get it back up to the nest.

"Okay, we can do this." I found some soft moss with my free hand and made a comfy space for the baby bird in the pocket of my yellow Mac.

"Okay." Down on all fours I brushed my hands over the forest floor searching for a worm or anything I could find as a peace offering. The earthy smell was a comfort to me as my own nerves started to kick in. I didn't want to hurt the baby bird.

"Aha!" A tiny slug-already dead, but still fresh enough for a hungry little bird family to eat. In my pocket it went. Along with a couple of woodlice –

"Sorry little guys." I apologised to the bugs before carefully climbing back up to the low branch. The little family of birds still frantically tweeted for their missing sibling. I drew together a bundle of leaves, moss and lichen, scooping it all around the little bird so as not to touch it with my hands. I gently placed him behind his brothers and sisters who would hopefully protect him from himself next time. I pinched the slug between my fingers and held it to the end of the highest reaching hungry beak. Sensing the offering, another of the babies opened its mouth, and in the little slug went. I did the same with the last two bugs I'd collected.

"There we go. Your mum will never know the mischief you got into today." I smiled thinking the same of myself being up in the tree. Mum always hated watching me climb. She was terrified of ever seeing me fall.

"What are you doing up there?" Came a voice from below. It was the white haired, grey eyed boy that had whispered to Obeah in the congregation space that first day.

"Just exploring. What's it to you?" I replied more harshly than I had intended. He was a tall eleven-year-old with an air of authority he didn't seem to deserve. His gaze was harsh and intrusive, his forehead frozen into a frown.

"I'm Obeah's nephew, head boy at school. I require you to begin joining us there each day if you're planning on staying here."

"Don't worry I'm not." I smiled trying to be a bit friendlier than I had started off.

"You won't find anything interesting up here. Its' just green and brown mush." He was so wrong. And quite rude, he looked me up and down with his nose turned up slightly like inspecting a bad smell. I didn't like him at all. I realised the familial connection then. Justin was Camille's son, the one she had tried to introduce me to the day we arrived. I'm glad Dad rescued me from that.

The next day I found a delightful old hazel tree with arms reaching from low on its trunk right up towards the stars. The tree was high upon a hill, I stayed sat in it until dusk. I saw red foxes starting to creep out of their burrows, grey squirrels played chase above my head, not even noticing I was an alien in their world. Little beetles with inky blue-green wings and nosey little pincers lived within the fibres of the tree bark. There was plenty to discover here. I liked watching the way of things, trying to work out what the creatures would do next. Buzzards lived quietly alongside jackdaws in the treetops. Different species of birds all living quite peacefully in the same space. I learned that they all used the same technique to land on a branch; their flying bodies would switch from horizontal to almost completely upright. This seemed to slow them for an efficient landing. Their little talons reached beyond their body aiming at their chosen spot, trusting that their aim was perfect. They never missed.

This was the day that I really started to miss being at sea. Dad had asked me to respect the island custom to avoid swimming. The islanders believed that it was not human to swim, their *'Sky Ones'* would not like to see humans trying to be fish, it was idolizing a lower creature - according to them and their *Book of Sky*. To me, the *Book of Sky* seemed to be a book of rules that only benefited Obeah. As the governor and 'chosen one' he took all animal produce first. Any left would move through the community from men, to women and children last. The reason for this was that his health was of the utmost importance in keeping a through line of communication with the *Sky Ones*. These were bird Gods that watched over the land, keeping the balance between good and evil. The rules of the island didn't affect me much, but not swimming? That was too hard. Dad had warned me to obey though, as a matter of respect *and* safety. 'It's far colder than you are used to. You might end up with cold water shock – especially if you go jumping in from a height. Just hold on a few more days please?'

Dad knew how I hated pointless rules. He promised never to push any on me – he never said, but I think he hated following pointless rules as much as I did. This request though, was about respecting places where we did not belong, and had not been invited. I did my best to follow the rule not to swim, because it was for Dad – I really did try. On this day though, watching the birds doing as they pleased, and the squirrels playing happily, I felt I was owed the same freedom. My heart was in the sea, and I had been trying to ignore it all week. Mum always said we should listen to our heart – 'it knows much more than our head pretends to.' She would say. So, listening to my heart I walked carefully down the valley. Old wet leaves made my pathway soft and slippery. It was almost dark, I knew I wouldn't have long before Mum called out for me. *Just a quick dip.* The air was cool and fresh. Little brooks were peppered throughout the forest, each one creating a baby tributary, a pathway to the river *Kunda* that ran through the centre of the island and into the sea. This was said to be home of the angry serpent Goddess or monster, depending on Obeah's mood. He'd switch from one to the other. Nothing was going to put me off the idea of swimming though, not even that. Mum had read to me about her from the *Book of Sky* – a gift from Obeah. She'd offered to read it to me as a bedtime story, but I switched off at all of the rules it had opened with; No swimming, no dancing, no listening to drum music, no singing and no chanting of anything other than the prayers offered from *The Sky Ones*. Boring.

The only 'sky ones' I was interested in were the stars that Dad had taught me so much about. To know that a star I could look at during any clear night, may have died and disappeared from existence hundreds of years ago, and yet, the light had only just reached my eyes. This was mind-blowing and magnificent enough for me. Why would a star care if I swam, or danced, or sang? I always thought they'd quite enjoy the show. I wasn't afraid of the water, or any creature that might lurk within its depths. Probably because I didn't believe in monsters yet. I followed the flow of the river, dipping my hand into a little brook along the way. Now this water was seriously cold. I wasn't ready for fresh water swimming just yet, I kept following the river down to the sea.

Crows began to gather in the treetops over head cawing their day's stories and deciding where they would set up camp that night. It was a comfort knowing I wasn't alone, as unafraid as I was. I found a small bay. It was six or so meters of clean sandy shore hiding in the shadows of large, exposed trees, their branches worn back and disfigured by the harsh winds of the open ocean. This secret spot was on the east side. I knew easily because this was where the sun rose from each day. As I got closer, this part was now in complete darkness. It was a waxing gibbous moon, which meant that the half-moon face was lit enough to show me the way out of the cover of trees. As the tiny bay opened its doors to me, the moonlight cast a rippling light across the water's surface. It looked like that line led into eternity. It seemed to have no end point.

I kicked off my wellies- I had never had to wear them so often in my life. The sand was soft and cold beneath my feet, and at last I could smell the salt. It was a different kind of saltiness, the colder air made it seem fresher somehow, light. At last ocean air filling up my lungs, and seeping into my skin. My hair had never been so soft, I was ready for it to go back to its sea weedy ways. Knots and all. I stripped off the suffocating raincoat, and the same red dress I had been wearing all week – even my pants. It was just me after all. I ran and shrieked with the crows into the shallow water and straight in up to my shoulders. The cold instantly took my breath away. I gasped, and laughed, and smiled brightly at the moon. For a brief moment I was home. The cold water tingled and slapped at my skin, it reminded me that I was alive. Slippery seaweed started to brush its silky palms over my legs as I swam in small circles counting to sixty in my head. It was the best minute I had, had since arriving on Sedna island. And then on the wind-

"Anwen!" It wasn't just Mum, but several voices. *Uh-oh*. I waded as quickly as I could to shore. I shook my whole body, hips, arms, shoulders, head. Like a dog shaking out its fur. That was the best I could do. I scrabbled to get dressed – struggling with my wellies most of all, they seemed to be fighting against me. Their rubber sticky against my wet feet.

"Anwen!" I ran back up the leafy hill, panting, my legs felt like jelly as they struggled to warm up and run at the same time.

"Coming." I shouted, hoping to allay their worries. Up to the peak, and down the other side. I could see the light of their lanterns coming straight for me between the trees.

"I'm here." I waved my arms over my head like the ship-wrecked under rescue.

"Anwen." Mum came running between the other four lights and dropped to her knees at my feet. She held my arms, her eyes glittering in the light of the moon. She was beautiful.

"Where have you been? We were so worried about you." Then Dad appeared, standing behind her. Our great mast.

"You've been swimming." His face darkened. I tried to reason with myself that it was the darkness of the night that did it. Dad never got angry with me.

"No, I... I was walking and I got lost, and I... I slipped-" There was no tricking him and I knew it.

"Come here-" He beckoned with a strong wide palm. Mum dropped her hands from my arms and stood aside for me to pass. Dad touched my hair, and then my coat.

"Your clothes are dry..." He rumbled. I nodded. "...and your hair is wet."

I looked down into the dark bed of leaves. My cheeks burned.

"I'm sorry." It came out as a whisper. The strangers behind the lanterns waited to see my moment of shame. Long enough for me to feel like burying myself in the forest floor like a hermit crab on the beach. Finally, they turned away and disappeared into the night. Mum and Dad remained quiet, as Dad looped a strong arm around my shoulder and lead me back down to our garden lodge.

"I'm really sorry Dad." He just looked at me blankly, which felt worse than if he had just shouted at me, to get the fight over with, so we could be friends again. I hated not being friends with Mum and Dad – it was rare, but it happened sometimes.

The inside of our lodge was a simple layout. A small open kitchen and living space shadowed by a platform only reachable by ladder. That's where we slept. On a shared mattress bundled in several blankets of all kinds of mismatching colours, and sizes. Everything was made from wood from the forests of this land. 'Made by the people of the island.' Obeah had boasted when showing us the space- 'We have all found ourselves washed up here in some way or another. I believe it's for a reason.' He smiled brightly then, and I noticed he locked eyes with Mum. She looked back and smiled. It wasn't her usual confident smile, but a shy smile that made her hide behind her hair and her eyelashes a little. It was the smile she gave Dad when he told her she was pretty. It was odd. Apart from Obeah and all his strange comments and unreadable looks, I liked our temporary home. The smell of wood meant that the walls here didn't make me feel too claustrophobic, or too far away from the sky and the trees. A big blue green, patterned rug almost covered the whole floor of the place. It reminded me of my ocean home and my bedroom with three portholes looking out to the horizon back on Shelagh. Dad had guessed we'd be here a week maximum, we'd already exceeded that and I was itching to leave. On day nine he pulled his promise from beneath my feet.

5

Chapter 5

There wasn't anything particularly odd about bedtime the night of my forbidden swim. There were a couple of strange looks between Mum and Dad, but I thought that was some shared disappointment in my breaking their trust. Dad went off for his nightcap, while Mum snuggled in next to me to tell stories from her imagination. All my books were on the boat and I had refused to hear any more from *The Book of Sky* and all its wrathful bird Gods. The islanders were afraid of birds, unsure of which were earth bounds and which were spies from another realm. As Mum's soft voice lulled me near to sleep, I asked her the question that I asked her every night for as far back as I could remember;

"What will happen tomorrow Mum?" She smiled her kind and lovely smile, with just a dusting of sadness at its edges. She stroked a wisp of freshly salted hair from my face and said her same answer that she always said.

"I wish I knew my little minnow. I wish I knew." Except this one time, she did know some of tomorrow's story, which I learned quickly on waking the next day.

As soon as the sun's light started to cast out across the far wall of the cabin, dancing upon my eyelids, I jumped up feeling sprightly after my swim. Mum and Dad were already sat at the table around a plate of buttered toast. We hadn't officially been invited to communal meals yet. They didn't notice me coming down the ladder at first. They were whispering, the floor creaked as I stepped down onto it, and they both turned to look at me. Their silence seemed to make a moment stretch out like an elastic band waiting to go 'ping'. I sat down at the table, took a piece of toast and poured myself some water.

"Morning." I said, as they both stared at me blankly like I was a stranger.

"What?" I asked suddenly panicked.

"Anwen..." Mum said with a dip in her tone, like someone is going to tell you your goldfish has died in the night. Like they are trying to brace you for something unwanted.

"Anwen, Dad wants to report this island discovery direct to Europa. This will be the next trip-"

"-Amazing. When can we leave this weird place?" I can remember myself smiling and the twinkling feeling of excitement in my belly.

"Well," Mum looked to Dad, but his head was bowed to the tabletop.

"I had been feeling a little low before we landed here. It's been a relief for me to be around such a tight knit community. This place reminds me of my home village..." I think this was the moment I began to realise where this was going.

"Dad and I, we both have a different outlook on family life, and this place has revealed a lot to me. So, so on this occasion you and I are going to stay behind while Dad goes on his expedition."

"What? What are you talking about? We're a team. We do everything together-"

"-We are a team, but we have split desires right now-"

"- What about my desires? I hate it here. Dad? This is a joke, right? You wouldn't leave me here with the black and white brigade."

"Anwen, I'm so sorry. Your mother has made up her mind, and daughters need their mothers. I will only be a few weeks. It's a great chance to map changes in the stars from a new perspective. This will be a well-paid discovery too. It will mean we can all take some time off on land together when I come back. We can pick anywhere on the map and just go. A real holiday – no work, no maps, no shutting myself away with books and compasses for hours on end. Just us."

"I can't face three weeks straight at sea right now my girl. The storm was so scary. I feel afraid to cross the continent when the weather patterns have become so unpredictable." Mum's eyes were welling up.

"Well, what about Dad? So, we just leave him to sail all alone? That's not fair."

"I'll be Okay sweetheart. Look how amazing Shelagh did in the biggest storm that has hit this part of the world in decades. She's a strong old girl. I'll be fine."

"I want to go with you." I mumbled the words and my cheeks burned with the shame of them. I knew they would wound my mother. But they were true. My dad was my true hero. He was the one who held the wisdom of the sky. He told the best stories, the scarier, unedited stories that Mum tried to protect me from. He was burly and strong. His eyes were my safety net – they held certainty in their depths. Mum was flightier, her moods would often turn inward, and she would go quiet and thoughtful. She was an island herself during those times, it made me feel unsure of the world, like a boat with no anchor. Her moods would rise and fall like the sun and the stars. When Mum was happy she was electric, she would energise everyone around her. But Dad had always said her worrying started when I was born. When her worries took over, she would often go sad and quiet, retreating to her sketch book or sleep.

"I just want to do what's right Anwen. I want you to have a safe and settled life. That might be here, it might not, but Sedna Island is safer than the sea."

The best thing about being a kid is climbing trees easily, and not having to clean up after dinner. The worst thing about being a kid, is not having a choice over where you will live.

6

Chapter 6

A few days later, Dad left. He handed me my knapsack filled with my five favourite books; A world atlas, *The Stars Night by Night, The Little Mermaid, Peter Pan* and *The Jungle Book*. The bag was as heavy as my heart felt, sagging into my stomach at this horrible plan. I knew that Dad only ever did what he thought to be noble and true – so I bit my lip hard and tried my best to trust him. He pulled me in, hugged me tight to his broad chest. His arms locked around me like the safe embrace of a nest to its egg. It was too fleeting a moment, as we both tried to hide our tears from one another. I'd never seen him cry before. Then he was gone, waving from my sailboat home and promising to be back soon.

That's when things quickly went from bad to worse. Those first few days brought on a turbulence of emotion in me. My rebellious side truly found its place in my mind, and I started with a few simple crimes. Casually walking over Obeah's flower beds was the first, that one went pretty much unnoticed, although Mum did bring it up at dinner that evening. Now that we were staying for longer than first expected we joined the communal dinner which took place underneath a great wooden canopy in the woods behind Obeah's garden. It was a beautiful space, the skeleton of a room; wood pillars holding a wood beamed ceiling. The whole structure built from carved wood, each beam still holding the shape of the tree it had once been, now smoother and cleaner, moulded by human manipulation. It was a different kind of beauty to the majestic, untouched tree stood up on its roots, but it was beautiful all the same. Beneath the canopy there was a long wooden bench that stretched far enough to fit fifty people, twenty five on one side, twenty five on the other. There was another taller bench that served as the preparation area, where the family that had cooked that day would bring the contents of their meal and begin to share it out into the wood carved bowls that had also been made by the islanders. Dinners were mostly soups and broths, breakfasts different takes on milks and cheeses from Obeah's goats. We all sat down that first communal meal together, adults on one side of the long wooden bench, children on the other – the balance not quite perfectly weighted, which was an unexpected irritation to me – to see there was a far bigger ratio of adults to children. Mum was sat next to Obeah. I was sat opposite Mum.

"I noticed the roses seem to have been trampled by something Obeah." She said casually to him, and quickly flashed a look to me. All the children sat together opposite the adults except for Justin. He was sat next to Obeah at the table; leader in training. They didn't look related at all, Obeah's head shaved, his dark skin versus Justin's bright white hair grown long enough to tuck behind his ears. His pale skin making his bright blue eyes seem menacing somehow, glowing out of his face. Both wore a crisp white shirt and red scarf. That was where their similarity ended. Obeah sipped at his broth, thoughtful about my mother's announcement of his crushed flowers. I learned quickly that he was very protective of his garden. Impulsively I took an opportunity to goad, retaliating to Mum's accusing look.

"What a shame. They were so beautiful." I said smirking at Mum. He dabbed at his mouth with a napkin and placed it on the table.

"Yes Anwen, a terrible shame. They haven't bloomed quite so well in a long time. And all thanks to your careful attention Laura…" He nodded and smiled at Mum.

"…Perhaps it was me in my rush to get out after breakfast. I took a short cut to the caves for Sunday prayer before sermon. My profuse apologies." He bowed his head and raised his eyes to meet my stare, smiling back.

"Yes, you really have made the garden lovely mother. Father would be very proud if he were here." I continued to hold Obeah's stare.

"Lower your eyes, you're being rude." Snapped Justin. The shock of being called out rocked my confidence. I could feel all eyes upon me, from up and down the long dining table – everybody had now seen me chastised by Justin. My cheeks burned.

"I don't think she meant any harm dear Justin." Mum tried to placate him in her gentle way. My embarrassment mixed with an achy feeling of love for her in my chest. It created a turbulence in my belly that made me feel sick. It made it hard to stay angry at her.

I decided to try a little harder at mischief by untying Obeah's goats from their posts. He kept six goats all to himself in his huge private garden. No one else had any animals, just Obeah.

Obeah decided who had earned their milk and cheese, and who hadn't. It didn't seem to be a choice made fairly. It seemed a choice he made out of vanity, favouring the family that had flattered him the most, or brought him the nicest produce from their garden. *Well I'll show him* I thought. I needn't have crushed the roses, for the black and white goat with the most enthusiastic buck ate almost everything. The other five made a run for it and no one could find them for days. Of course I made sure that nobody saw me do it, so no one could place the crime on my shoulders. Obeah called for an urgent meeting in the congregation space. He took to his lectern, and I stared past him at the poor silver birch trunk forced to listen to all this human, instead of the birds singing outside. Obeah asked all families to separate into groups and form a search for the goats. Camille and Justin stood proudly behind him nodding along with his instructions.

"If we aren't able to loop them on rope, we shall have to waste valuable grain to try and coax them back. If they take themselves off the edge of a cliff we will have lost an extremely important source of food. I don't want to have to sail to land to save us all. I can't keep rescuing you my people. You must rescue yourselves. Eyes are watching. Kunda awaits." Camille smiled up at him admiringly, but Justin spent the whole time with his gaze fixed on me. He did look priestly with the white shirt and red scarf, his lifted chin gave the impression that he looked out over people, when really he was smaller than all the adults he tried to cling to. I met his stare. I wasn't afraid of him. Then I yawned, and looked away catching the eye of Egret, the red haired girl that had dropped her tray that first day, and she giggled.

By nightfall on the fourth day of searching, the goats were

found and all was well on Sedna Island once more. When we got into bed that night Mum spoke first.

"I know the flowers were you Anwen." A long silence rested between us in the dark.

"The roses, and then the goats." She went on. "This can't carry on. Your father would be so disappointed."

"Well he isn't here." Was all I could bring myself to say. A lump caught in my throat.

"He'll be back, and when he comes I don't want him to find us segregated up there on the hills. I don't want him to know we have brought bad feeling between us and the people of the island." She whispered as if this were my bedtime story. This speech of hers.

"I'm bored here. I want to swim. I want to sail." I replied flatly. Mum wrapped her arm across my body. I needed the warmth now the nights were getting colder.

"Help me fit in here Anwen. The islanders are wary of us now. I want to make friends…It's time you made some too. School soon hmmm?" I deemed this a selfish and absurd request. I pushed her arm off me and moved my body away and closer to the edge of the bed. Then I lay wondering *segregated on what hills?*

A few days passed without event, wandering the same area of forest to sit on the eastern bay and watch the sea. I started writing letters asking to be rescued. I folded the pieces of paper into the shape of birds, like Dad had taught me, and let them float off upon the water's surface. I never expected anyone to ever read them. I knew the sea would swallow them first. Then, a couple of days later boredom got the better of me again.

During the daytime the children went to school in the congregation space, and the adults either tended their small garden plots, or they would cook together under the eating canopy behind Obeah's grand home. I knew once the flag was hoisted, that all the people of Sedna Island were busy with their tasks. That haunting image of the crow atop the snake was me cue to 'go'. I snuck into the far corner of Obeah's garden. It was a huge wide open space; enough land to hold the nine cottages and the congregation space easily. It had little hidden corners where he kept different beauties; the goats were one, the flower garden another and then there was a fruit garden. Mum had mentioned it as a place that was forbidden. That's how I knew it would be the setting for my next adventure.

I kept to the edge of the green and slipped through a gate. Rows of fruit trees opened up. Pear trees, apple trees, and strawberry plants laid out before me like a cave of treasure. It was far too cold for them all to look so full and ripe, yet there they stood. The roots were all covered in an odd coloured soil, dark red and shimmering. Obeah didn't share from his fruit garden. I knew because, of all this abundance, I had not seen one piece of fruit at any of the meals so far. I made a small hammock with the hem of my skirt and filled it with Obeah's strawberries.

"What are you doing up here?" It was Obeah's deep rumbling voice. His ice cold stare fixed on me. He glanced at my fruit filled skirt.

"Do not eat those." He ordered. In defiance, I took three strawberries in my hand and ate.

"I am done playing games Anwen. You are filled with darkness, like a *Zetalenda* – like a witch." I knew that word, I remembered it from Nelawi. My father had worked there many times throughout my childhood.

"Nelawi?" I said automatically.

41

"Come here." It was the first time he'd shown any emotion other than jollity. It was the first time he had let his mask of kind, fathering leadership slip. I knew he was a fake all along, but now he was giving me solid proof. He pulled me out of the garden and closed the gate. I hugged my fruit filled skirt against me as I regained my balance away from the scene of my crime. Shocked, I stood frozen to the spot. He disappeared, and quickly returned marching back to me with Mum by his side.

"Discipline. Real discipline is the only way to tame her. You must *tame* her to save her from the *Sky Ones*. To save her from the same fate as the people of the hills- the Outlanders." He shouted and gestured with his arms thrown out wide.

"Unruly hearts will drop into the realm of sorrow. That's where people like her end up. They never come back. Look-" Obeah paused his passionate speech and pointed to the trees

"-They are watching, they are always watching. I am the only one that can see, the only one that can appease them. That's how I keep you all safe. You must *tame* her Laura." Obeah looked around the garden and then left Mum's side, he went to the flower garden and returned with a bamboo cane. It began to rain, and the smell of wet grass calmed me as my heart rate began to rise. I slowed my breath. Obeah handed the cane to Mum.

"She will be better off in school, but if you wish this wild lifestyle for her, then you must punish her theft. Theft is against our laws. I should send you both to the hills right now." Mum's brow furrowed as her two truths were sent clashing and colliding for space and recognition, both opposing in their story. Her first truth - her love for me, and the second, her desperate need to belong somewhere. She wanted one clear truth, but found herself torn between angel and devil without knowing who was who. Then Camille came out from Obeah's grand house.

"What's wrong cousin?"

"It would seem we have a thief among us." Obeah raised his chin, like a raging bull set ready to charge, for the first time, he revealed an aggressive, intimidating side. A trait he had tried to hide, but I had somehow sensed it was there all along. It was in his eyes, his practiced mannerisms; the way he spoke so eloquently with his arms as well as his words, it was like a dance – a performance. This was the *real* Obeah. This was the side that everyone on the island was afraid of.

"She's not a thief Obeah. This has all been a terrible mistake. Our family, we have been to places where wild fruit is available freely to all. All a person need do is pick it."Mum pleaded.

"Are you questioning my authority Laura?"

"No, no…" She shook her head quickly correcting her path "…What I'm saying is that Anwen didn't know any better. She's not a thief. She's a good child. A beautiful child." Mum looked at me as she said it, her eyes searching mine, darting wildly. I felt her fear, and it made me all the more angry at her. Because she let my dad go and he would never have been afraid of Obeah like she was. He would have taken us all with him and we would be free again.

"Anwen, please just drop the strawberries will you?" Mum pleaded with me this time. The first strawberries I had eaten had started to make me feel woozy, my mouth was tingling now – numb. But I couldn't let *them*, Obeah and Camille, win. I took a handful of strawberries and shoved them in my mouth, chewing quickly. I let the rest drop. Mum gasped. Obeah stared at me. Dizziness struck, I broke into a sweat. And then

I fainted.

7

Chapter 7

I woke up hours later in our rainbow blanket bed. Mum was sat by my side holding a cold flannel to my head.

"You have a fever." She smiled. "It's just as well, because that was a sticky situation you got us into." Mum's smile faded, and she stroked my arm which was resting on my belly. In that moment, I couldn't remember what 'sticky situation' Mum meant. My mind felt foggy. I couldn't think straight.

"I miss Dad." Were the only words I felt sure of. I noticed then, that Mum had started wearing the black dress that all the other islanders wore. I hated it. It made her look pale and weak, her hair tied back. It was like she was erasing our old life fibre by fibre.

"He will be back soon. This place could be beautiful if you let it Anwen. Aren't the forests wonderful, so filled with life. These people worship the birds in the trees, they are dedicated to the land."

"The all think the birds are spies, there only to catch them out and punish them. That's not what Gods would actually do." My voice was flat and lifeless I felt so tired.

"It's not for us to question the intention of Gods or Holy men like Obeah. Stop fretting now. Try and sleep." That was an instruction I was able to take easily.

*

I had never set foot in a school in my life, and now it had been decided that I would go to one that told me what I had to wear; an outfit with the least amount of colour and the largest amount of discomfort. I was given a starched white shirt that was stiff and restrictive around my arms, and at first, an itchy wool skirt – when I told mum

"If you ask me to wear that I will shred it with the kitchen knife." She knew I wasn't joking and asked that Obeah allow me to wear shorts. They were still itchy and uncomfortable – but at least I could throw a cartwheel with complete disregard for my pants. I tried the whole thing on and stood at the kitchen table where she was sat waiting, I gave her my most miserable face, turning my eyeballs toward the ceiling and pouting my lips until my chin ached.

"Oh Anwen, I feel certain that you will forget all about the clothes once you are inside. The children all seem so friendly here. It will do you good to make some new friends. It must be so boring being surrounded by adults all the time." She smiled, her soft uncertain smile and squeezed my hand in reassurance. She was totally wrong about my friendship with adults, because the adults that Mum and Dad befriended were only the greatest kind of adults the world had to offer.

There was the Lord Parkinson of Betaland. He was a giant of a man with bright red hair to his elbows and a bright red beard which reached a point just above the belt of the kilts he preferred to wear. He wore a banjo across his body at all times and only answered serious questions in song form. He was a blast, and his songs were very wise, and often educational. Like, *The Whale that got Away* and *Why do Humans like Animal Tusks*. Then there was the princess of Nelawi, she was a falconer. She dressed like a pirate and had a new bird on her shoulder for each of the seven days of the week. Although she was a princess, she treated her people as equals, no one went hungry on the island of Nelawi. I was certain that the black and white uniformed kids of Sedna Island had no way to compete. I told Mum just that.

"I hate making friends with kids, especially kids that have no interest in playing outside. I haven't seen a single one of these island children playing in any of the gardens or in the forest. All they do is go to school and walk home each day. They act like automaton. What good is a friend that doesn't want to play?" I was sulking. I was definitely *not* feeling afraid.

"Well perhaps they will teach you about their way of life and you can teach them about yours."

"Why are you making me do this?"

"Because I want what's best for you. I want you to have an education. To have a proper home, and a proper family. I want you to have a normal life." She dropped my hand then and went to the kitchen to start preparing food for the community breakfast, a salad of goat's cheese and tomatoes.

"This place is not normal." I went and stood by her side, not wanting her to ignore my pleads.

"Let's try and give it a chance. It's just for a while. See it as a trial."

I agreed because I loved her. And because she told me it would be fine, and I trusted her. But Mum didn't really know what went on at 'school'.

Justin was the school prefect. As well as being unusually tall for a eleven-year-old, he was also unusually mean. It was his job to enforce the rule of silence while the teachers read from the *Book of Sky*. He didn't seem to have much enforcing to actually do, as all of the fifteen children sat bolt upright and perfectly quiet. But Justin walked up and down the line making a metronome with a stick of bamboo thumping rhythmically on one hand. He lightly whacked it on his palm in a 4/4 rhythm. It was his threat to the room. He was ghostly pale against his white blond hair and grey blue eyes. There was something other worldly about him. He wore a constant smirk on his face. I promised Dad I would never use the word 'hate' but I severely disliked this boy.

While the room was clearly too afraid to cross him, there was another way to experience his wrath. I got to see first-hand on that first day at school. Everyone looked the same here, all wearing the same black and white uniforms, all only differing in age by a year or two.

I'd asked Obeah, in those first days, about the matching everything. He'd explained it as a measure of equality. 'A man should not be defined by what he owns, or how expensive the silk upon his back may be.' I did understand the theory. But why black and white? Couldn't he have picked a more cheery colour?

We were all sat on the floor cross legged. I recognised Egret and Thomas from that first day. Bot sat together, bolt upright. Thomas' dark hair swept across his forehead masking one eye, Egret's beautiful auburn curls, the colour of autumn leaves, was all bound up into a bun on top of her head. I caught Egret's eye then and smiled. She looked away. She was stocky like a rugby player, but she had a gentle face. An elderly man was our teacher, he was the oldest person I'd seen on the island so far.

His body bent forward, no longer able to straighten his spine, his glasses were thick and yet he still seemed to be struggling to see. He held *The Book of Sky* right up to his nose, his eyes squinting at the strain of his site.

"Where there is no guidance, a people falls...But in the counsel of the chosen One we find safety. Beacrow, God of the sky is angry, having had this island stolen by Kunda, Goddess of the sea. Our dear Obeah is the mediator, the chosen One, keeping the peace between the two. Ensuring the skies are fed with prayer and the dedication of all the people of this land...working together to keep this land alive...controlling Kunda's insatiable hunger. In this way of life we hold off earthquakes and storms and will someday be welcomed into the realms of the *Sky Ones* where we will live eternally free and at peace. Free from pain, free from hunger, free from fear. Surely that is worth the toil children? Surely that is worth the toil." His voice wobbled on and on, even his voice box was tired of the repetition as it croaked and rasped at the effort of speech. It was an appealing thought. I would do anything to dull the pain in my chest every time I thought of my dad. It didn't explain why Obeah was the only one not to toil, or share his garden's offerings, or to decide who will become an outlander- whatever that was.

Egret sat quiet but allowed herself to slump into a position that advertised her disinterest. She gave into her boredom so completely, that she fell asleep. Her snores reverberated with a sudden crescendo as she simultaneously toppled over into Thomas.

"Hey." Was his automatic reaction. Egret fluttered back to life.

"Sorry Thomas." She whispered. Thomas was the one now

looking apologetic as the rest of the room spun to look at the commotion.

The one-hundred-year-old scrunched up teacher simply looked up at the sound. He stopped talking and cleared his throat with a loud cough, and a nod to Justin. Justin gladly loudened the thwacking of his bamboo cane on his palm as he walked across the line of children sat cross-legged on the floor. Egret had by now woken herself up and sat upright like the others staring directly at her fate.

"Egret Mullins, stand up." Justin ordered, and she did. "You have disrespected the sacred teaching space. Do you accept that this causes for punishment?" Justin had lifted his chin and stood taller, like he was some kind of sergeant major, his blue eyes twinkling- excited. Egret unconsciously rolled her eyes. She had seen this all before. She did not seem afraid, she simply held out her hand limply. She was uninterested in this fake authoritarian and his joy in causing pain. He raised the bamboo high over his head and cast it down upon poor Egret's hand with such a whipping force that a physical crack roared out into the domed ceiling. The whole room flinched in unison. But tough, smart Egret raised her chin and met Justin in height. Wow.

The rest of that morning I tried to absorb the stories of the *Sky Ones*, who seemed to be angry about everything. There were so many sins to learn of and avoid. It was overwhelming, and hard to believe.

Egret and I quickly became friends. She had a quiet, but shared disregard for the rules of the island. This was the glue that brought us firmly together. Skipping school was off the cards with a class of just fifteen, which meant our friendship time took place after hours. I learned that Egret's mother was sick, so her dad was glad to see her off playing with a new friend-even if it was the 'island outcast'. Our play had to look like work, we would pick potatoes in her garden and then sit cleaning them above a bowl of warm water. But we could whisper stories from our imagination, and talk of how we would rule our own island. We were also sometimes allowed to walk the forest so long as we returned with plenty of firewood.

Egret's father was a kind looking man that appeared older than he really was. He had a deep sadness about him. Our games of make believe became stories of plans to overthrow Obeah, and break his strange spell over everyone. It was just a game though - at first.

Most of the children went straight home after school to help with preparing the village meals. Egret was released from this while her mother was unwell. While each home and garden looked the same in the village, there was a subtle difference I learned once Egret explained it to me. Each garden grew different vegetables and herbs in order to keep some variety to the daily meals, all of which were prepared on rotation by a different family each day. We all had to come together to eat each day below the wooden canopy behind Obeah's home. We were warmed by fire, and the space lit by candles as Autumn took hold of the sky and the evenings were turning darker.

There was a small clearing I hadn't yet visited having become so enamoured with the eastern bay. Egret lead the way. There was a circle of trees where we could collect our firewood, kick up dry red-brown leaves and play without eyes upon us. Up on a hill in the distance there were three fields, distinguishable from afar by the colour of their land. Like a patchwork quilt, they were adjoined rectangles of yellow, green and brown. Egret taught me that the brown field was for sweet potatoes, the yellow field was filled with wheat, and the green field was for corn. There were people working up there.

"They work the fields every day. They live up there." Explained Egret.

"But why? Why don't they live in the village with you?" Once I had seen them for the first time I couldn't unsee them. Once my eyes had attuned to the small figures on the face of the land, I could see the rhythmic swinging of bodies working scythes. The slow monotonous push of a plough and another handful of bodies always bent over on hands and knees in the brown field picking the potatoes. They were easy to see really, for they did not wear the black and white uniform of the islanders. The land workers wore beige linen coveralls. It was a haunting backdrop to the village. They looked a lot like ghosts if I stared at them long enough.

"They are the *outlanders*. Members of the community that did not obey *The Book of Sky*. Many of them are related to one another. They will work the land up there until they have burned away their 'frivolity' as Obeah names it." Egret shrugged.

The size and shape of their bodies was a mixture of small and lean, large and broad. They were men and women, both working side by side, with a couple of bodies that looked small enough to be children.

"Do they ever come down?"

"No. Look." Egret pointed to two wooden huts at the lower edge of the hill. "They all live in there together. They are not permitted to be a part of the village until Obeah receives the sign that they have repented. And they get to eat very little of what they harvest."

"Well, what if Obeah never receives a sign?" This was almost too strange to bare. *Does no one care about them?* I wondered. Egret seemed not to, she was used to the way of things here.

"Then they stay there. Here, I got one of these…" she threw me a red apple and winked.

"Is this from-"

"-Shhh." She put a finger to her lips and we both laughed.

"There's a doctor up there." She said then as she laid back and began to eat her stolen apple. I laid on the grass next to her and stared up at a cloudless blue sky. Comforted that I could still see into infinity even if I didn't feel I could reach out and touch it any more. Egret took another bite and continued talking as she chewed (an offence in Obeah's presence).

"Dad said that Obeah should let him come down. That the only offence he ever committed was to share his intellect. Obeah says that Doctors just mess with the plan set out by *The Sky Ones*." We both lay in silence eating our apples and probably thinking the same thing – Egret's mum really needed a doctor.

"But if the man was already a doctor and Obeah had to discover it, then that means that he came from the outside world like me?"

"Erm, I don't know. I guess."

"So not every islander was born here? There are hardly any older people."

"I was born here. I don't know much about how the grownups arrived. Dad told me a story once, but I can't remember it. My memories are often just blurry blankets of time that just… don't exist anymore."

"That's so odd. I feel like my memory of my dad is fading." She turned her head to look at me while I spoke. "I can't really see his face in my mind any more, just his dark beard and the yellow hat he often wore."

"I'm sorry to hear that Anwen." Apples finished. "Come on we should go." Said Egret, we scooped up some sticks and dry leaves on the way back to the eating canopy.

At dinner everyone was in their familiar place at the table, children on one side, adults on the other. I took a new tact and raised my hand to speak.

"What is it Anwen?" Mum looked perturbed as I had never used such formal manners before.

"I'd like to ask Obeah a question if I may?" Obeah sipped at his broth, still steaming. He looked up and down the table, all eyes upon him, nervous. A child should never be so forward I had gathered by the palpable fear.

"Go ahead." He nodded with that cold eyed smile of his.

"How did this community begin? I mean, there are no elders here, so you must be settlers?" Obeah coughed almost spitting his food across the table at a blond girl named Darcia who was looking down at her bowl. He dabbed at the corners of his mouth with his handkerchief, and adjusted the red scarf tied at his neck.

"What a question. Well, yes we are settlers I suppose. I piloted a plane that crashed here, and we began our lives anew like a serpent shedding their skin, like the goddess Kunda until she fell out of favour with the Gods."

"Why?" I prodded. He laughed his bellowing laugh at me than.

"Well child, that is what your schooling is for. Listen close, and you will learn all the stories of this land." The adults looked up and down the table at one another, the children kept their eyes lowered to the table, Justin stared at me, looking furious as he always did. We all fell into silence for the rest of the meal.

*

Eight weeks passed. We had still heard nothing from Dad. He had estimated that his trip would take one week each way, with a month spent in Europa to see a full moon cycle through the sky. Weather depending. The only radio signal and access to electricity the island had, came from Obeah's house. He and Mum had been spending more and more time together. So, it seemed reasonable that she should ask him to radio for any news of bad weather along the route Dad had planned to take.

The evening of the day I'd asked her about it, I was sat at the kitchen table waiting for her to come home from her chores, which were all jobs based around working Obeah's private gardens. It was just as the sun was slipping down behind the trees, the owls began to hoot and the bats began to flit and twirl across the dusky blue sky. I'd spent the early evening writing my SOS letters to release as paper birds into the choppier Autumn waves. I was alone, Egret had to help her father with food preparations for the coming days breakfast. As soon as I got home I'd started a fire to warm the room. Mum returned with one arm holding a basket filled with potatoes and the other hugging a pile of rhubarb against her waist. She smiled when she saw me at the log burner, her face flushed from a day outdoors. A lot of what we ate back on Shelagh was tinned or cooked from frozen. Especially if we were at sea for longer stretches. Mum was clearly enjoying her newfound land legs.

"Did you ask Obeah about radioing forward for Dad?" I stood and asked before she had a chance to lay anything out on the table. Her face dropped at once.

"I did." She walked over the ocean coloured rug and set her day's finds on the floor, then pulled me in for a hug. My cheek squished to her chest, and she said

55

"Obeah lost radio connection in the storm right before we arrived. He is trying to fix it, but we have no means to communicate right now."

"But I've heard the wireless playing out news reports-" She took my face in her hands and lifted it so that she could take me in, our eyes locked. I was trying to plead from inside. *Please can we go find Dad.*

"Obeah listens to music and spoken word on a record player. That's what you've heard." She assured me.

"As soon as its fixed. He will call us up to the house."

"He's lying." The words came out before they'd even touched my mind. Unexpected but what I felt to be true from somewhere deep in my belly.

"Anwen, Obeah is a good man, a kind man. He wouldn't lie about such a thing."

"How can you be so sure?" The fire crackling broke the silence first. We just stood staring at each other. She was trying to read me as she always did when she couldn't understand me.

"Because I have no reason not to trust him Anwen. I don't remember your father giving us a timescale for his trip."

"He did it was the last thing he'd talked through the morning he left." I insisted. She had that disappointed face that I hated so much

"I'm sorry, I don't remember that. I do wonder what reason you have not to trust Obeah though? He has been very good to us – to me."

"Just a feeling." I shrugged, feeling every bit the child, with nothing else to offer.

"A feeling?" She shook her head and picked up the basket of potatoes and rhubarb. She put them by the sink and started washing the vegetables.

"At least pretend you care about Dad." I shouted. And I left the house slamming the door behind me.

I knew Egret's house. It was at the end of the row of identical houses, each with their identical looking vegetable gardens. Her front garden was slightly more neglected than the others with her mum being too poorly to tend to it. I snuck up the path and crouched at one of the windows. I could see her at the kitchen sink, washing dishes. Behind her, a make-do bed that seemed to home a bundle of blankets, but I knew it was her mother. I tapped the window softly and she looked up right away, as if she knew I was there all along. I waved her to come out. She shouted something over her shoulder and then joined me out in the garden.

"What do you want?"

"Someone to play with?"

"Play? Play What?"

"Forest adventures?" I shrugged. She looked over her shoulder again and said

"Okay." I lead her up the hill and through the small gap in the thicket to take us down to my secret cove.

"How did you find this place?"

"By looking around. Don't you people do that here?"

"Not really we're all kept pretty busy."

"How's your mum?" I asked.

"She's okay." We sat at the top of the hidden path that would lead us to the sand. Egret's eyes saddened.

"What's wrong with her?"

"We don't know. She just doesn't seem to be getting any better. At first we thought it was just flu, but her lungs, they just...they don't seem to be filling up as she sucks at air."

"Will your father ask Obeah take her to the mainland?" I

asked. She looked down at her shiny black school shoes and shook her head.

"Obeah only travels alone in a food emergency. Nobody else knows where the 'mainland' is. No one here remembers anything but this place. Just look out at the horizon, there's nothing as far as the eye can see."

"I'm sorry." I said again. "Do you know how to skim stones?" I changed the subject. She shook her head. It was almost dark now.

"Come on. I'll show you." I stood up and brushed the dried leaves from my scratchy school shorts.

"I can't be too long."

"I know." I smiled and held her hand as I lead her between prickly gorse bushes. We crunched over the fallen autumn leaves down to the tiny beach. I picked a smooth pebble for each of us. We stood side by side at the edge of the water.

"You have to flick your wrist like this." I showed her.

"Wow." She said, as my stone bounced across the glassy surface seven times. Circular patterns rippled out like little explosions.

"Winner is the one that makes the most bounces across the water's surface." I said.

"Okay." She threw her first stone, it landed in one heavy plop. We both laughed.

"Like this." I showed her again, exaggerating the flick of my wrist. And that's how Egret became my first proper best friend – throwing stones, sharing in success and laughing at our failures. We got back to the village before complete darkness. I snuck inside the door and up the ladder into bed next to Mum. She wrapped her arm over my shoulder and moulded my body into hers.

"Aren't you going to ask me what happens tomorrow?" She whispered sweetly into my ear.

"Not anymore." Our collective sadness filled the air like a heavy fog. I was unable to see a way through it.

Chapter 8

I played sick for a week to get out of school. I'm not sure if Mum really believed me, maybe it was an easy way to keep both me and Obeah happy. Each morning that week Mum would bring me some warm milk in bed, kiss my forehead and leave. I'd climb back into my soft cotton dress, douse its red in my green wool jumper so as not to be seen so easily, and then pop on my wellies ready for my next mission.

I started to spy on Mum and Obeah. Every day before sneaking up to the forest,

I would leave the lodge and hide behind the back wall until Mum was out of sight. Then I would take to the hedgerow surrounding Obeah's garden and sit watching whatever I could see from there. Obeah did the same thing each day; Find Mum a new job in his garden and then bring her a drink.

"Apple juice." He smiled on the first morning. "It's a commodity here, so you are a lucky lady. But I think you will find it relaxes you." I watched her take a sip and smile at its sweetness. The one thing Mum and I did have in common was our love for anything sweet. I was saddened to see how keen

Mum was to please Obeah. I'd never seen her so subservient. As that week wore on, Obeah and Mum started to sit on the bench by the rose bushes to drink their juice together. I was so angry at her for getting on with a life without Dad. I was able to weave deep enough into the hedges and sit behind them to listen.

"You should start coming to the evening sermons now you're staying longer term. It will help with the loss of your husband." *What? Had she given up on Dad already?*

"I will. I will join them soon." She did sound sad at talk of Dad.

"It will guide you in the raising of Anwen." They fell silent, and I held my breath not wanting to miss a single word. A twig crunched under my boots and Mum looked over her shoulder. Obeah cleared his throat-

"She's a special girl." His words were hollow.

"Yes." Mum agreed.

"But she is wild. *The Sky Ones* suggest that the only way to realise our destiny is through discipline and toil." 'Flattery', Dad had once said, when I was feeling nervous about meeting the head of the Serbian army, 'is the best way to build an instant connection with a stranger.' Was this what Obeah was doing with Mum? By calling me special? He'd only ever regarded me with a wooden smile and a terse politeness that seemed more like hidden disdain. A manner that he seemed to take with all the children of the island. I had to get us away from here. Obeah was slowly pulling Mum into his orbit, placing her under his spell. Mum was in a tug of war; Obeah at one end and me at the other. With mum and I arguing, he was on the winning end. I listened to him go on.

"*The Sky Ones* offer us freedom of Spirit through dedication to them. But it must be exclusive. It's the only way to cement our souls in an eternity of blissful tomorrows." I wanted to jump up and scream. 'You're wrong. You're talking of the powers of the universe, of the stars, and the sun and black holes! They don't care about our toil. They're too busy expanding.' I knew if I revealed myself, I would only make Mum angry that I'd been spying.

So, I took to the forest. It was time to make a real plan. I was going to get us off the island, we would sail us to Europa and find Dad.

There were other beaches scattered at each corner of the island. I needed to start visiting all of them and increase my origami rescue letters to the sea. It was a hopeful whim, an attempt to feel as though I were doing something towards finding Dad and getting away from the increasingly cold, grey skies of Sedna Island. No other idea would come just yet, there was no boat – I could build one? No map – find Orion's belt and keep it on the left? A mother that didn't want to leave? Folding paper birds with wishes felt like a start. I took the little white squares and wrote

Please help. We are stranded. Currently,
12th October, we sit east of constellation Cygnus.
North of Vega.
Something strange has power here. I am the
Daughter of Guy McQueen,
Missing cartographer.
Come quickly.
Yours Truly
Anwen McQueen

I folded the square of paper in several directions making

the creases I needed, then I bent the body into shape, folding the corners into wings, and peeling the front into a head. I did this five more times, and across the course of that week's feigned illness, I sent a paper bird swimming out to sea with my hope filled words. The southern beach was the one that we had arrived on to begin with, the one where Dad had spent his days fixing Shelagh, and the beach that he eventually left us from. It was the main harbour for any incoming or outgoing trade. Although I hadn't seen or heard of any such trade since arriving, but Egret said so. This beach was less isolated than the others, the soft white sand was peppered with clumps of dried-up seaweed, black and sharp under bare feet – my preferred way to travel.

Looking at the island from the sea it still looked like an unbreakable line of trees, but I had learned the quiet pathways through to the central village, and all the animal hollows through low lying bushes. I imagined that from above, the island must have looked a lot liked a compass; with a beach at North, South, East and West, and two secret coves in between. My favourite swim spot, at the eastern beach was the place I was most familiar with, though I hadn't dared swim for weeks. Egret would have known she could find me there when she was sent to the house with herbs for me, only to find it empty.

When Egret did find me that Friday afternoon, I was scouring the front line of trees for broken branches; these would make up my escape raft. A loud crunch from behind me had me turn with a start. At once Egret and I screamed each startling the other..

"Egret, what are you doing here? Isn't it school hours?" She stayed quiet. Her eyes were red, and her muddied face showed streaks of dry tears like river tributaries. She held her left palm open to me revealing three parallel gashes that might have looked less painful if they had simply bled. Instead, they had turned into horrible swollen welts.

"Oh my gosh Egret." I held the back of her injured hand in both my palms gently, like some fragile creature. It was the middle of the day and feeling more like winter with the sun low in the sky and giving off little warmth. I shivered and rubbed at my arms waiting for her to speak.

"Even Mr John looked sorry this time. I think that's why he sent me to your house with these herbs." She pulled a paper bag from her skirt pocket and handed it to me. I could smell the familiar scent of eucalyptus.

"Thank you." I said, and then asked "What happened?"

"Justin has been getting nastier with everyone in class this week, but especially me. Since you and I have become friends." She averted her eyes from me then, looking at the floor.

"That's awful." I felt heavy at the thought.

"I'm not going back. I've told Dad about it. If it's not the cane, it's the nasty words about my hair, and the questioning of my dedication to the work of the *Sky Ones*."

"You have a right to choose your own thoughts, everyone does. He has no right to treat you this way."

"Sadly, he does. It's actually his job to scorn, and hurt and break anyone that steps out of line."

"Do all the parents know what goes on there?"

"I think so. Obeah seems to justify it, and they seem to buy into what he says. Except-" She stopped immediately, pulling her hand away from me. It was as though the thought had burned her.

"What is it?" The only answer I got at first, was the sound of the waves, gently lapping at the shore.

"Egret?" I pushed. She bit her lip, which made her look unusually timid. Her eyes were searching, as she wrestled with the idea of releasing the thought out into the world.

"It's nothing. I won't get away with not attending school for long. But I guess I could catch your illness." She smiled weakly and nudged my shoulder.

"I don't understand why Obeah has so much power over everyone here Egret. What is it that makes everyone so afraid of him? To make the outlanders stay hidden up there." I gestured in the direction of the hills. Egret simply shrugged and shook her head.

"So he arrived by plane, we know that, and then what? He found *The Book of Sky*? Or did he write it? The people chose him to lead, or he chose himself?" I asked desperately feeling the frustration rise in my belly like a tsunami ready to attack the shore.

"Well he was chosen by Beacrow, the King of the sky Gods, father of *The Sky Ones.* That's what we are taught. We are not allowed to ask too many questions, but-"

"But what Egret?"

"It's nothing, I just – I know my mother was born here but Dad has never explained his past. His memory is blurred... although..." She wanted to tell me something more, I knew.

"You can trust me Egret. I won't tell anyone anything that you say... If you don't want me to." She nodded once, her decision made.

"Dad is usually so unrelenting when I complain about school. He has never shown any sign of budging on the matter. Mum was the same..." She pressed her right foot down into a pile of dry seaweed and tangled sticks between us. Twisting and scrunching in thought.

"But since… well, obviously Mum is so sick, and Dad is doing his best to care for her. So, he is tired and sad. But there's something else-"

"What? What is it Egret?"

"Since missing the last four sermons in a row, it's like a cloud has lifted from Dad's way with me. Something in him has softened. Even his eyes seem less cloudy, less glazed over. It's like, like some spell has been lifted."

"Oh my…" A penny was dropping.

"What?"

"Weirdly, I believe it. It's felt like everyone here is under some weird spell. I've thought it from the very moment we got here. It's all so strange; the houses, uniforms, the unwavering dedication to Obeah and *The Sky Ones*. Not a single other belief system allowed. Obeah isn't *that* kind either, or warm in any way. He's like stone."

"That doesn't give us any conclusion. He is an odd man. A scary man. His mood can change at the drop of a hat. You haven't seen him really angry yet. That's why anyone named an outlander just goes – gladly. I sometimes envy them." She looked down at her poor whipped hand and brushed a finger gently over the wound. We carried on walking along the forest wall of trees, picking up only the largest fallen branches.

"Well, I'm leaving." I said over my shoulder. "We are powerless to change anything here. I need to get to land and get help to find my dad. He would never just leave us here and not return unless something has happened. I believe my dad is in danger, and I'm starting to feel like we all might be too." At my mention of danger a thick grey cloud began rolling towards us from the sea, a rumble of thunder cracked out into the sky and rain began to pelt down onto the surface of the sea.

It rolled slowly towards us.

"Quick get under cover." I shouted, and the two of us ran under the thick canopy of hazel trees that lead to the path. I dropped my pile of sticks. We both stopped still, turned back to the water and watched.

"*The Sky Ones*." Whispered Egret. As the cloud and the rain met the line of the land, it suddenly stopped. Not a drop of rain touched the sand, the dark heavy cloud lightened and passed gently over us. It was as if the cloud was trying to tell us something. It was on our side that's for sure – why else skip over our heads. Then I started to think that maybe this place was starting to blur my thinking like everyone else's. Egret broke the silence first.

"You can't leave." I turned to look at her, as we both walked back out on the beach. She was older than me, but in that moment, she looked so childlike.

"You're my only true friend here apart from Thomas. I don't know what I would do without you. And Mum…" The words choked her, she hiccupped back a sob, her eyes filling with salty tears. I wrapped my arms around her shoulders. She was two heads higher than me, it was a comfort to hug her, even though I was the one throwing the hug.

"I think Mum's going to die."

"Then we'll get her a doctor too."

"How? It's impossible."

"Nothing is impossible."

"You are trying to make a raft of rotten old sticks." She laughed then, at the absurdityy of my idea. I looked around at the poor pickings from the morning's collecting, and I had to agree.

"Yeah, you're right. I will rethink the plan. I'm a sailor, if I

67

can't escape by sea then nobody can." I took her good hand and turned to walk back to the village with her.

"Ouch!" I cried out.

"What?" Egret looked panicked. I had stubbed my toe on something metal, glinting in the sunlight. I picked it up, it was a spanner – too clean and barely touched to have washed up there. There was no sign at all of salt water damage or sun burn.

"That's Obeah's." Egret said straight away.

"How do you know?"

"He's the only one on the island with any hard tools. He uses them to maintain radio signal, and the one boat that he has tucked away for himself… he was helping your dad fix Shelagh, wasn't he?"

"What? No."

"Oh, well that's what he said when he had come to visit my Mum when she first fell sick. It was a few days after you arrived." I knew in that moment that something was amiss. My dad would never have let a stranger work on Shelagh with him. He was the most protective man I had ever seen. He loved that boat like she was a member of our family. If there was ever a problem he didn't understand, he reluctantly sought out professional help. Even then, he would interrogate the person like they were some kind of criminal before letting them near Shelagh. He and Obeah had not liked each other, that was obvious to all of us. Even Mum and Dad had argued about him the first few nights into our stay.

The memory that came to me was a night when Mum had gone out for a walk. She didn't mention meeting Obeah. When she returned home, Dad and I had been sat at the table waiting, three plates of steaming vegetables set out. She sat down and I had asked

"How was your walk?"

"Great." She said with a bright smile and rosy cheeks

"Actually, Obeah has offered to fix the boat engine for you." She announced brightly.

"What experience does he have with boats?" Dad asked sat bolt upright.

"Well, none with boats, he was a pilot before arriving here so he has worked with plane engines."

"Planes aren't boats are they?" Dad had snapped.

"Why are you being so short?" Mum was mirroring Dad's rigid posture then.

"You never said you were going walking with the leader of the pack."

"Did I need to?" Mum retorted, and the stone throwing went on from there. The back and forth, it was like watching a game of aggressive tennis, where each player hits the ball so fast you can barely follow what's going on. I didn't see this between Mum and Dad ever on the boat. The island did strange things to them. I could see no reality where Dad would have allowed Obeah near our boat.

"Obeah has a boat?" I asked Egret as this fact pulled my attention back from the panic of a nastier realisation.

"Well, yes, it's only small but, it's what we would rely on if Obeah ever decided to go to the mainland. I can't remember a time that he ever has."

"Where is the mainland?"

"I told you before, I have no idea. No one has the faintest clue of what lays beyond life here." Egret's brow furrowed as if she was trying to grasp at a memory that wouldn't materialise.

69

Like a butterfly, truth fluttered away here. We walked a few steps further, and another strange piece of metal was poking out from the sand. It was embedded in a deeper layer of wet sand and stuck hard. Egret and I crouched down either side of the sharp jutting corner. We dug with our hands finding flat edges of what appeared to be some kind of box. Once we had dug deep enough, we pulled out what I recognised at once, to be the transistor radio from Shelagh. It was the inner box exposing all the vital parts that would keep Dad in touch with the rest of the world. He could have gone two days at sea without noticing with its main carcass left in place down in his office below deck. That, along with Obeah's spanner, was enough to tell me everything I needed to know, and everything I didn't want to know at the same time. This was my dad's lifeline. This was my dad's only means to communicate from the boat. Wherever he was now he had no way of being found by anybody on land, or in the sky. If he was lost in the ocean, he was possibly lost forever.

"I have to get away from here." Were the only words that would come out of my mouth. Egret simply looked at me, not quite understanding what was going on.

"Where does Obeah keep his boat?" I asked.

"It's at the North West side of the island. There's no way to it by foot. He makes a big deal about how strong a swimmer he is. And how he should be the only one to ever try to swim to it. The only other way to it by land is a sheer drop of cliffs. It's all jagged rock face. It's the harshest side of the island. You would never get anywhere near it if that's what you're thinking." She must have recognised the idea as I stood up quickly. Holding the spanner tight in my left hand gripping my dad's radio under my right arm.

"I have to go." I said and marched away from Egret leaving her stood behind me looking helpless, her injured hand resting limply at her side. She called out after me

"Anwen, I wish it were possible to change things... really I do- I just... We have no power, we are children. What can we possibly do? If Obeah discovered us, he'd make us outcasts, sending us up to the farmlands to toil and starve, and be tortured for the rest of our days."

"We can outsmart him. He would never expect that anyone would try and take the boat. You are all so afraid of the sea."

"But he knows you swim. That's probably why he wanted rid of your father. Anyone unafraid of the sea is a threat to his power. Anyone going back to the real world is a threat. Your father was going to report the findings of a secret island wasn't he? If the world arrived at Obeah's door, I'm not sure what would happen. He was afraid of what your father woulf bring here, of that I am sure. The outside world cannot find him."

"Then we need to find a way to do just that – to get the outside world to come."

9

Chapter 9

I started to feel that odd sense of anticipation you get right before you place the final handful of puzzle pieces into their carefully shaped holes. It was a constant mix of elation, downheartedness and frustration. Each emotion whirled and fluctuated across the push and pull of the tides each day. I felt elation at having made the decision to escape, and frustration, because I really felt onto something with Obeah and his baffling control over the islanders. I knew now that there must be a reason for everyone having such a limited memory of the past. It was time for one final mission before my sickness story lost its weight with Mum. There was one last thing I could think to try to piece it all together. I went to the fields of the outlanders.

I followed the thin forest pathway I had taken with Egret. It began behind the congregation space. I managed to find my way back to the clearing of trees where Egret and I had enjoyed our forbidden apples. After finding my way to this spot the fields became like a mirage. Every time I thought I'd found a walkway that lead to them, I'd arrive at a dead end. A parting of trees would become an unbreachable hedgerow of tight knit gorse, heather or hawthorn. It was as if the land had been intricately crafted to behave as a labyrinth, keeping the two peoples of Sedna Island easily segregated. I couldn't let it defeat me that quickly. I walked the wide circumference of the aggressive hedgerow. It felt much more threatening now the flowers had gone to seed and all the thorns and spikes were on display like little soldiers ready to take on their attackers. This outer pathway circled itself upward, and before I knew it, I was above the living huts that Egret had pointed out to me that day. I noticed then, a low lying opening that lead to an underground burrow – a big badger home. I got down onto all fours and desperately wriggled my way into the gap between the hedges. My belly was pressed tight against the cold muddy floor, my hips could barely lift enough for my knees to dig into the ground and shift me forward. I felt like a very incapable caterpillar. My hair and my green knitted jumper were snagging on the sharp branches and thorns. I could smell the earth and all of its eternal composting, wet and musty.

"Ow." My breath was shallow and my mind frantic as I suddenly began to question my choice to intrude like this. I worried *what if I'm not welcome here? What if they take me prisoner? Or worse, send me marching straight back down to Obeah to be exposed?*

Once I'd pulled through the four to five feet of nightmare, I scrambled to a stand brushing off my elbows and knees and shaking out my hair.

"Hello."

"Aah!" I screamed as a girl slightly younger than me appeared from nowhere. Her hair was dishevelled – the way I preferred mine to be. Her eyes were bright and joyful at her discovery.

Her beige overalls were stained and threadbare, her cheek bones more prominent than any child's should be.

"What are you doing here?"She asked in a panicked whisper.

"I need some help." I whispered in return. The girl's face darkened then.

"No one here can help you. You better leave before someone sees you. They won't be as kind as me. We aren't meant to mix with islanders." The girl turned to walk away, her head bowed in sadness.

"Wait." I grabbed her arm to stop her "I'm not an islander. My family washed up here a couple of months ago. My father left to report his findings, but I believe Obeah sabotaged his trip. I believe Obeah to be a fraud…but I need to prove it. I want to leave this place and bring back help, but I don't know how." The girl stood frozen to the spot, her head cocked slightly towards me. She was listening.

"Can you help me? Will anyone up here be able to help me?" I asked desperately. The skinny young girl turned to face me.

"Does anyone know you're here? Anyone at all?" I shook my head.

"Wait here." She ordered before scampering away down a winding pathway that disappeared behind the first hut. A few minutes later she returned. She was running and looking back over her shoulder.

"Can you climb?" She asked.

"Of course I can." I shrugged.

"Follow me." She took me to the base of an ancient hazel tree, its tear drop leaves blowing gently on the wind making a soft song of the sky. The trunk was so wide, it would have taken the open arms of three children to hug it. Like a star fish, it sent five equally thick branches outward in different directions, each forming a bridge-like structure. They were only a few feet above the leafy forest floor, so I followed easily, apart from the girl's incredible speed – she nimbly hopped any knots in the wood, any little of shoots of branches that formed a kind of obstacle course, as she showed me the way to a small hidden cottage nestled within a dense circle of trees. The chimney smoked. Inside the room was sparse, a woman sat on a wooden stool by the fire. Her hair was blond, curly and wild like Mum's had been, my breath caught in my throat at the similarity of her to *old* Mum, as she had been before the island. She was washing a pair of overalls in a bucket of water by the fireplace. She herself was wearing a green dress. She saw me looking at her clothes.

"Oh, I only wear these in here. Wouldn't want to be seen out of uniform." She looked down into the water and carried on rubbing the fabric between her hands, a lather building, she spoke as she worked.

"So, you're here to save us all are you?" I could see a smirk creep upon her cheek though I was side on. It was playful.

"I want to take Obeah's sailboat and find land." I stated confidently, though it was the first time a concrete idea had revealed itself to me.

"Oh?" She stopped what she was doing then and turned to look at me. "That sounds like a silly idea. Where will you head?"

"My dad is Guy McQueen, celestial cartographer, I will try and follow the stars." She nodded slowly taking me in, the girl that brought me there stood quietly in the corner of the room. The warmth of the fire started to heat my cheeks, I was feeling flustered. Trying to look like a person that had a plan, and not a helpless child which is how I started to feel, stood talking to a stranger about an escape plan that didn't actually exist.

"I know that Obeah is hiding something, I just cannot believe that any God would have chosen him to rule this place. He is selfish of heart." I tried to speak up, but my voice faltered. The beautiful outlander lady rung out the overalls she'd been scrubbing and hung them above the hearth. She turned on the stool to face me, she glanced across at the girl who had found me.

"Anita come here." She said holding out her hand to the girl – Anita.

"You did the right thing to bring her here." She turned to look at me again and beckoned me closer.

"What's your name brave heart?"

"Anwen, Miss." I replied.

"You can call me Joaney. I know of your father. He was quite famous back when…" She stopped and looked away, unable to go on, she cleared her throat.

"Before. Before we arrived here."

"So there *was* a life before this place. No one down there can remember anything, or won't reveal it. They are all so filled with fear and fog of mind. There are no Gods are there? It's all a lie."

"Oh there are Gods." Joaney nodded thoughtfully. Yes, there are. I was the one chosen to paint the flag that flies each day above the congregation space. Obeah ordered it that Beacrow the bird God of *The Sky Ones* to look as though he were slaying Kunda, goddess of the sea. I was a painter before." She trailed off again, at any mention of 'before'.

"So, the image on the flag is a lie?"

"Oh yes. This is Kunda's island, her home. I don't know how Obeah has manipulated the magic of this land to serve himself. But I know he has her under his control. He has starved her out, feeding her just once a year... Well, we're all better off up here when that happens. Beacrow was our protector as we travelled. He remains stuck in the heavens above us because his duty to protect is incomplete. Obeah changed everything. That's all I can tell you."

"If you all know the truth, why haven't you left? Why haven't you tried to stop him?" I felt more confused than ever. Joaney looked at Anita and stroked her arms.

"We are safer to just keep ourselves busy up here. I would never do anything to risk my daughter's life. That's how we all feel. The land to that boat is dangerous. I'm not even sure Obeah has ever sailed. Claiming the boat as his is a threat of no escape. He has kept it out of his own fear of being stuck here forever- that's what I believe anyway There were more but... well, they were taken by those that lived here before. If you made it up here through all that gorse, you can probably find a way to get to the boat. But it won't be easy." She reached out and took my hand too, myself and Anita stood side by side, one of our hands each held in hers. We could have been sisters, Anita and I. We were the same height.

"None of us can sail. None of us can navigate. That's why it's never been worth the risk of trying to leave. The boat is small, it would carry just a handful of us, and even then we might be running to our death. But you Anwen, you could be the key. His power lies in the land somehow. He is so protective of that garden. Find his source of power and then we can snuff it out. He will never suspect you to be brave enough." She searched my eyes.

"I'm not sure about that." I whispered. I had already caused so much trouble.

"I can see courage in your eyes." She smiled at me then. "I

miss painting. He cast me up here because he knew that I knew his story was a lie. That's the only reason. He told me an artist's mind was an untrustworthy one. He's superstitious about that flag. The flag comes down, his faith will rock. If you are seen anywhere near this place you and your family will be in danger. You must go back now. The boat can be accessed from the Western cliffs. Be careful." Joaney hugged me tight and I felt myself soften into her embrace. I wanted to stay there in her arms by the fire. Fear of what was to come filled my legs making them feel less able to stand.

"Show Anwen the simplest way back down to the village Anita." Scruffy Anita nodded and took my hand. The cool air hit me as soon as we left the cottage, it was a relief, it steadied my nerves. I breathed it in deeply, taking in the smell of burning wood, salty air and hope.

Anita lead me back down to the village. Once the congregation space could be seen above the trees she turned and ran back up the hill without a 'goodbye'.

"Thank you." I whispered. As I turned the corner to the front of the building I nearly had a heart attack for the second time that afternoon.

"Thomas! What are you doing here?" I gasped. He spoke and signed as he had done any time we'd interacted so far. His hands gesturing in sync with his words.

"It's my turn to raise the flag before sermon tonight. What are you doing here?"

"Wait, Thomas, can you hear me?" He flipped his head upward to clear his floppy dark hair from covering his right eye.

"Yes of course." He answered using sign language as he spoke again.

"Then why do you sign?" I tried to gesture with my own hands as I spoke.

"Oh this?" He looked down at his hands, his cheeks a little flushed "It's a force of habit now." He held his arms down by his sides, conscious of my gaze upon him. "I used to be deaf, I was born without sound, but Obeah cured me." He smiled, shy.

"I'm not making fun, I love it. I wish I knew how to talk with my hands too." I reassured him. "How did Obeah cure you?" I asked curious. Thomas shrugged.

"Pouring his blessed wine into each ear apparently, that's what gran tells me anyway. I was a baby."

"Oh." *The wine he gives at sermon*, I thought.

"Thomas?" I asked coyly, he now had the power to blow my cover and I really needed him not to. Not now.

"Yes?" His cheeks blushed again.

"I'm working on something really important, and Mum thinks I'm at home in bed – poorly. I'm not asking you to lie...but-"

"But?"

"But, can you just pretend you haven't seen me today. Just... don't mention it specifically to anyone?" I shrugged my shoulders to me ears, held tight onto my breath and pleaded with my eyes. Thomas didn't speak, he just made a circle with his thumb and index finger, signing 'Okay'. Then we both went our separate ways.

10

Chapter 10

For a reason that I could not explain even to myself, I chose not to tell mum about the radio. I got back to the house that afternoon to find it empty, as I often did. I went to the cupboard beneath the sink in the kitchen. A place where we rarely needed to go. A place where only soaps, old rags and cloths were kept. I pushed the radio and the spanner far back into the cupboard, covered them with some of the dusty old cloths, and went up to the bedroom. I opened my knapsack and pulled out the books that Dad had left me. The only access to information outside the poison that Obeah was feeding everyone. There had to be a reason for his lust for power here. He didn't want people to swim, he wanted them to spend all their free time tending gardens that produced only a small crop for each household. It was a life on repeat. But he was the king of it.

I pulled out the world atlas we had picked up from a flea market in Jujaden Bay. Dad paid hardly anything for it, and yet it felt to me, like the most precious thing a young girl could own. It was the largest book I had, always weighing me down when

I carried it around with me in my bag. But it was too precious to leave alone here on this island. I slid myself under the bed of rainbow blankets. This way, if I heard Mum coming, I could hide everything away very quickly. I opened the atlas and began to scan through the pages. Its gnarled edges were a comfort to me. For a very brief and fleeting moment, it felt like I might be on my own bedroom floor, back on Shelagh. I was trying to work out our navigation pathways. When we travelled with Dad as our captain, he would start by looking at his *Mercator chart*, which is a map with lots of measurements already taken, to help sailors figure out how far they need to travel to get to their destination. He would then pull out another chart, called the gnomic ocean chart, to double check the distances he had calculated using his single handed divider – which looks a lot like a mathematical compass used for drawing perfect circles. I had none of those things. But I hoped that somehow if I could figure out a direction, any direction that was heading towards a mainland, and if I could hold that line by following a star path, maybe, just maybe I would make a safe passage to somewhere. I hoped I would find someone that could help over throw Obeah's power.

"I will show Egret that it can be done." I whispered to myself as I tried to come up with an impossible plan.

I opened the first pages to stare at some images the atlas called the continental mosaic. These were flat images of the globe taking the shape of wide oblongs, staggered across two pages. I wanted to work out where this island was on that huge globe of space. Looking at the place where Shelagh was approximately located, before the storm hit, was my start point. But where to go from there? I really had no idea. It could be anywhere. There was no specific wind direction I could fathom out of the chaos that day. As soon as the storm took a hold of us we were blind. Victims to the wind. Washed up unknowingly in this colder, harsher climate. From the Chaudarian sea, I had to assume that we had been pushed north. The lower temperatures and the cooler weather conditions suggested that we were definitely northern hemisphere. This narrowed my search by fifty percent. There was no land in sight standing at any high point on the island. However, from the most southerly point, there were often low lying clouds in the distance. Static and unmoving. I knew from Dad's navigation experience, that a static low lying cloud often meant land. This was my only starting point for deciding which direction to head. Next, I needed to plan how I would steal Obeah's boat by myself. It was a long swim, or the navigating of a dangerous cliff face. If only I had known that someone had been watching Egret and I on the beach that afternoon. I would not have bothered with the brainstorming session.

I hadn't ventured much to the west of the island so far because it was so hard to get to. Gorse bushes overlapped each other on this side of the island, much as it had when trying to reach the outlanders. They were all entwined and interconnected, a thorny army ready to defend its coastline. While I was certain it was great for stopping anyone coming in, it was also a horrible thing to navigate for anyone trying to get out. All the other corners of the island seemed to offer some kindness, some gap made by a creature never seen, a natural pathway to the sea for anyone curious enough to want to explore – although curiosity did not exist among these people. In my many hours spent wandering the island alone, I had attempted to make a knife. It was made from a broken pebble and a thick, angular stick. This gave it a look of being bent or broken, but the weird angle did seem to add to its power. I had bound the pebble to the stick using twine, it wasn't hugely sharp, but it was huge. It could possibly pass as a baby axe if I had to classify it in a book. I tried to hack at the gorse branches to make a way through. The yellow flowers had long disappeared. And the hacking proved unsuccessful. My arms and legs were scraped and stung by the fight with the sharp thorns of the gorse bushes. I felt determined not to let the sting beat me.

Giving up on the gorse route, I decided to climb one of the thicker oaks in the forest. I had hoped that to get to higher ground, I might see a way through. I was a competent climber. If I could just get a good view of the cliff face from above, I felt sure I would be able to plan the safest route to the boat. I left my bag at the bottom of the tree and found some good holds in the giant knots of this beautiful beast. My right foot did slip on a loose piece of bark just once, it gave my knee a good skinning. I could feel warm blood trickling down my shin. The cool air soothed it. Once at the highest branch able to support my weight, I looked across to the west side of the island. The gorse rolled on and on, thick and heavy for at least three hundred metres before I could spot a small line of marsh that led to the edge of the land.

"Damn." I climbed down the tree even more carefully than I had climbed up. Just then I heard a crack followed by complete silence. I knew straight away, it was no animal.

"Hello?" I called out. No answer came back, but I knew someone was there. Their silence told me they weren't on my team. I stayed still a moment, trying to gather my thoughts and calm my nerves as adrenaline started to pump making my whole body thrum and my mind sharpen – but there was no easy escape, nowhere to run to from here. My only option would be to face whoever was hiding. I pulled the baby axe from my pocket and climbed carefully down the backside of the tree, the side that was furthest from the sound.

"Hello Anwen."

"Aaah!" I spun to find Justin stood right in front of me, and now blocking my path of escape. I pressed my back into the thick trunk of the tree, and he took another step forward.

"Justin, what are you doing here?"

"I'm here to make sure you aren't about to do anything silly." His eyes narrowed and an evil smirk spread across his face. He knew he had me cornered. He did not care that I was smaller or weaker than him. He got great pleasure out of other people's fear.

"Well I'm just exploring. You said there was nothing to see in the forest, but there's plenty-"

"Including my uncle's boat huh?"

"No, I-"

"I know what you're up to Anwen. I've been watching you and your little friend Egret on the beach – plotting. Well your plan is foiled."

"Well then, I better head home." I shrugged nonchalantly.

"No." He pushed a palm into my chest forcing my back against the hard, jagged bark of the old oak tree. "You will do no such thing."

"What do you want from me Justin?"

"I want you to repent. I want you to obey the rules of this island. Your rebellion is causing quite a stir." His eyes narrowed in on me, his brow furrowed. It was a cold hard stare – those ice blue eyes, he was like a serpent about to bite.

"Then why not let me leave. Let me go and your island can go back to normal." He started to laugh then, loud and callous. There was a glint in his eyes, this excited him – the confrontation, the danger of it. He was as bored as the rest of them. He just acted it out in a different way. He edged a step closer, slowly, like a prowling cat.

"No one leaves the island Anwen. We are a family, remember?"

"But my dad–"

"-Your dad was going to be more trouble than you. Obeah could see that from the start. It was best that he took to his fate on the seabed." He smiled again, still pressing his hand hard against my chest and now he brought his nose to mine, his forehead pressing on my forehead. I could feel his hot breath on my face. Anger boiled from my belly as his words sank in and I snapped.

"Aaaarrrgghhhh!" I dived my whole body at him and swung my axe. Things blurred then but he toppled backwards, caught off guard. I continued to screech my war cry and swing the poorly propped axe at him as his crawled backward on the muddy ground. One swing caught him on the shoulder and he yelled out in pain. Scrambling now, the bully was afraid. A coward. As he got to his feet, he caught my axe mid swing and launched it into the air. Weapon gone, he ran back at me, shoving me to the ground now. I rolled out of his path and jumped up. I ran at him again, a rugby tackle. My height made my hit land perfectly at his waist and he bent double landing to the floor again. I sat on his chest and thumped the sides of his head like a mad person. Using the edges of my fists. He brought his arms up over his face yelling

"Get off. Get off me you lunatic. You're dead now you know that."

"I don't care." I screamed back. "You killed my dad. You all

85

killed him didn't you?" It was the first time I'd said my biggest fear aloud. It hurt more than anything this boy could do to me. He rolled out from under me, his momentum threw me off to the side. He got up and ran away shouting

"They're coming for you, everybody knows – you won't get near that boat. So give up now." I stayed there on the ground and sobbed into the leaves. I held my muddied bloody hands over my face and cried until Mum's voice brought me back from my grief.

"Anwen? What on earth is going on?"

"He's dead isn't he? They killed him Mum."

"Oh darling." She dropped to her knees, now adorning the black skirt and white shirt and apron like all the others. She scooped my body up onto her lap and hugged me tight to her chest.

"It is likely that Dad is lost at sea Anwen. I'm so sorry."

"It was *them* Mum *they* did it. Obeah sabotaged Dad's radio."

"Oh sweetheart no, he would never do such a thing. It will be okay Anwen, I promise it will-"

"-I want to leave here Mum *please*? Let us leave, it's poison, it's poison Mum."

"Shhh now, don't say that. Shh shh shh." She rocked me there for what felt like a long time. From all the fear, and the shock, and the panic the only thing I was good for now was sleep. When I woke up I was in an unfamiliar bed.

11

Chapter 11

I t was a room in Obeah's house. I knew because there was the man himself, sat at my bedside reciting some foreign tongue from his *Book of Sky*. I tried to sit up but my limbs would not obey me.

"What's going on?" Panic filled my veins once more.

"You're sick young one. I have served you some medicine that will help to calm you. I need you to get better now okay?"

"Where's Mum?" I whispered through my frozen lips.

"She's fetching herbs to soothe you. She will be back soon. Shh now." He continued chanting over me, his bass like voice haunting my mind. All the room was dark wood. The bed sheets pure white and cool against my scraped shins. I was in a night dress now, white with pink flowers. I could see the frills beneath my nose. Obeah droned on, and I squeezed my eyes shut and hummed, drowning him out. It was an incantation, he was a wizard, and everyone here was under his spell, including Mum. I was done for, unable to move under my own command. He poured a red liquid over my lips, just slightly parted, I felt it wash down my throat hot and burning. It was wine. It was the wine and his chanting paralysing me. It was the wine that he made from his fruit. The fruit not allowed for anyone else. The wine that he served the grown-ups and Justin every day and night at his sermons. My brain fogged and whirled at the realisation. I was being swallowed by a cold gripping fear of this devil by my bedside.

What I did not know until some time later, was that other children were starting to question the way of things. Egret had been sharing stories of my time on Shelagh, and a new craving for such wild freedom was spreading. Kids were realising that if they stayed away from the congregation space, their spirits would strengthen. Obeah's spell got weaker for every moment it was not cast out into people's ears. So kids started playing sick. Staying home. And this is what had Justin in such a wild panic. But in getting caught before finding the boat, I'd ruined any chance the island had at escaping Obeah's power.

As I lay in the bed, I realised It was over. He would never take his eyes off me now. I would never be able to think or breathe, or walk the forest without a pair of eyes on me. All the community would be watching now, not just Justin. Everyone. I had no choice but to succumb to his rule and go back to school. Obeah had won.

Mum came soon after his chanting. My humming had seemed to create some barrier between him and me, an imperceptible space, a bubble of protection. The tune I had hummed was an old sea shanty Dad would sing to me at night. It was called *Heart Armour*. When Mum came, I was calm. I now understood the game was more complex than before, but my only option, for now, was to play.

"Sip this my love. It's rosemary and lemon, it will calm you."
I did, and the warm perfumery upon my lips soothed me. I

relaxed my head back onto the pillow and sighed.

"I'm sorry Mum. I'm ready to go back to school now." She pulled her chair in closer to my bedside stroking my forehead. Obeah stood to leave. He was smiling. My limbs began to wake up.

"There can be no more fighting, okay?"

"I know." And I did agree with that. I could see no use in petty brawls with the likes of Justin. Mum was changing. I didn't recognise her. Her wild hair was tied back and tame. As was she. No one had any fight here. There was a clue in my humming though. I felt sure of that. My only contact with the outside world was through my letters of hope folded into tiny birds, and sent out to sea with little chance of survival. It felt like a hopeless act, but it was the only one I had left.

So, I went back to school. I behaved the way they wanted me to behave. I listened. I sat up straight. I pretended to repeat their chants, moving my lips without letting sound exit my throat. Because I had learned something in my humming of the heart armour sea shanty; Their words couldn't get me if I kept that humming quietly in my mind, rasping it almost silently at the back of my throat. Egret and I kept our distance. But communication can take many different forms.

Seven days of school passed in a long painful blur of time. There wasn't even a clock to watch to try and measure the start and the end of the day. Just the constant drone of an uninspired reader. But boredom can be a beautiful thing if you submit to it. Because the thought of escape and rebellion just built bigger and bigger in my mind. Like a snowball gathering size and momentum as it rolls on and on, so did the thought of overcoming this drudgery. My next plan suddenly revealed itself to me. I would need an army.

I began writing more letters. If we were being watched, there could be no visual sign of building friendships. I started the chain with Egret. It read

My Dear friend Egret,

I have learned some scary things. I think you will believe me when I tell you that we are all being placed under a spell. You are the only one I know I can trust. I have discovered a chant that behaves as protection. This song will keep your mind clear:

Soul farmer sing
You are heart's armour
Armour from selfish desire
Protect me from hell fire
May I be freed
From the threats of greed
Soul farmer sing
To me please bring
Heart armour
Heart armour
Soul farmer

Chant this quietly and often. Pass it on to those that wish to be free.
I am working on a plan.
I will need you.
Your friend always
Anwen

That letter held our only means of protection from the lies in *The Book of Sky,* and Obeah's unquestioned control over the people of the island. If we were found out now, none of the adults would believe us. Obeah would be able to overthrow our plan at the click of his evil fingers.

The island was quiet at night. No one ever wandered the

village or the forest. The night time became a way to live a secret existence. I was tempted to take more moonlit swims of course, but I could not risk my salty hair, or wet clothes, or sea smells that Mum would recognise in an instant. So I took the paths I knew best to the water. To the eastern bay of the island, and I continued to release my paper birds filled with hopes and prayers each night. I upped their frequency, letting out a new letter each night for seven nights. The only witnesses were the late summer crickets hanging on tight into Autumn, they sang and chirped as I released the carefully folded origami birds, the white of the paper glowing beneath the moon on clear nights – like miniature swans drifting off with my calls for help. Help from anyone that could come, from anyone that may know of a distant island where once a plane had crashed and never been found. This was the plane that had started Obeah's reign of the place. Someone out there must know the plane, someone must know this evil man from a past life. If the sea spirits really existed, I hoped so desperately that they would carry those letters to someone that might help us. Each letter gave my name, and my father's name. Many seafarers would know my father's name if they found a letter. I hoped his good name would make us worth saving. I started to try to map the island, to try and make a sky view picture in my mind.

Our loft bedroom had a trapdoor that lead out onto the roof. Mum was a deep sleeper. When I was not sneaking off to the beaches, I was climbing out onto the roof to watch the stars. Just like Dad and I had from Shelagh's deck. I couldn't believe I hadn't thought to turn to the stars sooner. On the first night I went up there, I knew straight away that we were absolutely Northern hemisphere. I could see Ursa Major and Ursa minor, each moving slowly across the night sky as this strange earth turned while I felt so stuck. Completely trapped on this tiny dot of land upon it. Those constellations are said to look like two polar bears, but to me they always looked more like kites. I could see Orion before long too, and I remembered Dad telling me that Orion was the one constellation you could rely upon when travelling by night. Its core stars seemed to remain static against other movement of the night sky. The air was so cold up on the roof, my breath turned to smoke rising up and up towards those twinkling diamonds in the sky. I wished so much that I could fly upward as easily as that. It was this thought that gave me the idea of flying to Obeah's boat, when the time was right to try and escape once more. Not in a crazy, wing making attempt like Icarus, but rather as a clever means of riding upon the wind – just like we did when sailing.

12

Chapter 12

So I needed a sail. Some kind of fabric, thick and durable but lightweight enough to be lifted by the wind. I could use it like a parachute to get to Obeah's boat. The idea came and went as ideas often do. Since the fight between Justin and I, he had seemed to disappear. He hadn't joined class since my return to school. Without him stalking the room like a predator moving between trees; watching and waiting for the perfect moment to strike, without that, everyone seemed to relax into themselves. Perhaps they were also getting ideas about escape, or maybe they were just happy not to have to sit so tall all the time; back's aching, necks tired. I couldn't decide who to share the heart armour with. All the children were so blank faced. I decided to take a risk on Thomas. Thomas was a boy that gave away everything in his face. His eyes would roll towards the stars when the teacher would make some brazen claim of the world ending, and of curses and sea monsters. He clearly had questioning in his heart. So I passed another note to Egret, who passed it to Thomas. It was easier to do without the watchful gaze of Justin. Following a quick nudge, Thomas took the note from behind Egret's back. I watched from behind them as he slipped it up his sleeve. Phew. I took this as a good sign.

That same afternoon I'd seen her pass the note to Thomas I checked in with Egret quietly as we left school for the day. Walking by her side I whispered

"How many notes have you given out?"

"Oh I've given one to everyone." She answered chest puffed up with pride.

"What? Egret-"

"-What? There aren't many of us are there? I figured we had nothing to lose and everything to gain."

"Oh my Goodness, this is all getting very real. Has anyone spoken with you about it?"

"Nope. They just take the note and hide it away. Maybe nobody's actually read it. But I had to try." She shrugged and then disappeared in her own direction towards home.

Justin did eventually come back. And when he did, he was filled with an even greater desire to cause suffering than before. Now he would pull children up for the cane for just a drift of attention. A distant stare, or a wandering gaze. The class would be sat in a study circle with ancient Mr. John at its centre, droning the words from the *Book of Sky*, Justin constantly stalking the perimeter until he found his prey. Just three days into his new, stronger reign, on a regular Wednesday morning his target was Thomas; our potential new ally.

"Thomas Pinaka stand up." He narrowed his eyes on poor Thomas who was tall and gangly, even more so as he towered above Justin. Thomas shook his head to get that dark hair out of his eyes as he often did. He looked calm, nonchalant even. Justin gave a satisfied sneer, just like he had with me in the woods.

"For not paying attention." He raised the cane up "Hold out your hand." And whack. This place was more how I imagined a prison than I ever imagined a school.

"And this-" Justin went on "-is for your attempt at treason…" Justin wrestled his hand inside his pocket and pulled out a scrunched up piece of paper. It was one of our notes. "Hold out your other hand Pinaka." Justin smirked as he lashed the cane down even harder on Thomas' second hand. Thomas gasped at that one, so did the rest of the room. All the other children started to look at one another. Each fearful that they may have been found out too.

"Sit down." Justin ordered Thomas, and he did. He stood in front of Mr John now. Without a care for the teacher's existence he barked

"This boy should be sent straight up to the fields of the outlanders. Maybe he will be – Obeah will deal with him in tonight's sermon. As for the rest of you, if you receive a note, you must hand it in immediately or meet the same fate as him. Do you understand?" The room looked on dumfounded, some children nodding absently.

"I said do you understand?" He repeated louder and with more aggression.

"Yes Justin." The rest of the children echoed in synchrony. My heart beat hard in my chest. Egret, sat just ahead of me, shuffled in a little tighter. Nobody spoke up. We had been lucky.

Thomas started to avoid Egret and I. It was a submission. We'd lost our first soldier. Being outsmarted by Justin once already had me paranoid. I bumped shoulders with Egret on the way out of school that day.

"I'm sorry..." I mouthed "...no more notes." She nodded in agreement and we parted.

It was just another of my many mistakes during this time in my life, though anything not fatal can at least teach you something about yourself. Those kids were brave enough to hold onto the secret, or maybe too afraid to share it. Either way, I lived to see another day - a whole lot more actually.

Three more weeks passed in a monotonous cycle of eat, sleep, sermon, repeat. Mum and I spent most of time together in silence now. It sat between us like a heavy boulder, leaving us less able to see, or relate to each other every day. I couldn't understand why she wouldn't speak of my dad, or push Obeah to radio for news. He had communication alright. I'd seen him up there in his secret room at night, the one where he'd laid me, and cast some trick to paralyse me after my fight with Justin. From my rooftop, in the dark of night, I could see his silhouette lit by candles as he held something to his ear; listening. Maybe he needed to know that the world out there had not discovered him yet, or maybe it was to follow the weather. Whatever reason he had to keep that thread of connection with the outside world, he wasn't about to share it with 'his people'.

My mind started to fall into despair. Despair about how I would ever leave this place, or find my dad, or even just get my mum back. Then a miraculous thing happened. It came with a gust of wind. This big idea that forced its way back into my mind. The flag that was hoisted each day as a reminder of the battle between sea and sky, a battle that Obeah held off with all of his 'spirit'. Well it began to billow and flap aggressively on the wind. A storm had begun to find its way inland. We were all piling out of the congregation space. I was walking alongside

Egret and Thomas when a loud bang came from above us. We all spun to see what it was. Even Justin let his tough facade fall for a moment as we all simultaneously ducked from some perceived threat. Then, like a fern unfurling in spring, the flag rolled out as the wind clashed with its thick canvas. As it did, a bolt of lightning struck the silver birch to which the flag was winched upon. Its ropes caught fire. There was a great commotion. We all stood there staring up at it.

"Save it!" Came Obeah's voice rumbling from up the hill where his house was. He must have been watching from the garden.

"Someone save it!" He bellowed again. This was my chance to make something right. I ran back inside the congregation space, and grabbed a bucket of water from the bathroom. I looped the bucket over my forearm and began to shinny up the silver birch flagpole. I made it to the ceiling quickly enough. It was just like being back on Shelagh for a split second. There was a trap door in the ceiling that was easily unhinged and flipped open with one strong push. I launched the bucket of water across the flames that were now licking up the ropes and towards the canvass of the flag. As though Beacrow himself were watching and routing for me, the heavens opened and rain began to pour down onto us. Everyone was outdoors now watching on.

"Well done Anwen!" Obeah shouted clapping and smiling. The first genuine smile I had ever seen from him, and I wondered if it was a ghost of someone he had been before all this.

"It is damaged." I called down. "I shall have to bring it down." Obeah looked around at the villagers who were all now watching him for his reaction.

"Okay." He nodded, but he looked nervous. It was as though we were frozen in time. Like the moment stretched out just long enough for me to realise the opportunity presented. My next move in the game needed to be carefully thought out.

That night Mum and I were forced into the house much earlier than usual. The weather had taken a turn for the worse. I sat at the table waiting for Mum to serve our first lone dinner in over a month. It felt good to be able to relax in one another's company now I'd served a good deed for Obeah. The tension eased slightly between us. I enjoyed watching her potter around without fear of the eyes upon her. I was enjoying the scent of rosemary, garlic and roast vegetables filling our less than new, land-bound home. I couldn't stop thinking about the flag, and how I could get it into my custody. As I sat there with the image of the bird and the sea snake whirling in my mind, a memory flickered. I'd seen a similar image before – it was a mural in a market square back on Nelawi. The place Dad and I had loved most out of all the other places we had travelled. In the mural though, there was no conflict, it was an image of hope. Sky and sea in alliance. Obeah had stolen the image and twisted its meaning.

Nelawi was an island we had visited for Dad to map the stars from the equator one summer. It was warm and jungle like there, filled with lush palms and colourful flowers of all shapes and sizes. We went to different places at different times of year back then, because the sky looks different depending on where the earth is in its cycle. But from the equator you get the widest views of the night sky. The people of the island worshipped nature in a way that made me excited to be around them. Even as an eight-year-old at the time, the people of the island almost out shone my own energy and zest for life. They would dance to drum music under the light of the full moon, and they would sing at the rising of the sun each day. They would celebrate each meal they ate with stories and hugs for those that had prepared it. As I remembered the place I ached. I would have done anything to be anywhere else but this cold and lonely island. If I'd been given the choice, I never would have parted from Shelagh or Dad.

I needed to get that fabric somehow, it was currently bundled in a pile in the congregation space. Obeah not trusting anyone to touch it. He took its destruction as a sign from somewhere, I could see that. He was losing his composure as he paced and circled around it like a father inspecting his injured pup. That night, shut away in the house just Mum and I – for such a long night, I realised that Mum would have the most sway with Obeah. She would cause the least suspicion in offering to bring the flag home and fix the ropes. I tucked into a dinner of buttered potatoes and garlic vegetables. Mum silently cut into her food across the aged wooden table. We had grown quiet and distant from one another these past weeks. Attending that school every day was more soul destroying than I cared to think about. It made resentment grow and fester in my belly. She no longer knew what to say to me. Her only questions of late had been 'how was school?' To which I would always reply with the same answer 'torturous'. So she stopped asking. But now I needed her skills more than her understanding. Unexpectedly, she spoke first.

"That was very brave of you today Anwen." She smiled softly, a curl had loosened itself from her tight ponytail in the heat of cooking. It softened her whole demeanour.

"Thank you." I smiled back, then turned to flattery as Dad had taught me.

"You were always the best at mounting masts." I added. We smiled at the memory of us all living and surviving together aboard Shelagh. My perfect life. Mum's smile dissipated quickly, something passed over her like a storm cloud. It blew her smile away and made her eyes look sad. It seemed like it might be a moment of realisation. But it passed too quickly to make anything of it.

"I'd like to offer to fix the flag. To re-tie it's ropes. A peace offering." She looked up from her plate, questioning.

"What?" I shrugged "It might get Justin to ease off everyone in school." This seemed a good enough reason to offer up. We carried on eating in silence. As we both cleared the plates and tidied everything away Mum said

"I will arrange to bring the flag home tomorrow. I think Obeah will be pleased to have some experienced helpers."

"Tomorrow." I repeated. The word that used to bring me so much wonder and mystery, now seemed to have no meaning. So predictable and lack lustre was my life here.

Just when I thought that life would remain predictable and stagnant forever more, Egret told me a story and Mum did me a good deed. The next school day was over in a blur, and as we all filtered out of the towering double doors like a miniature swarm of ants. Egret pulled me out of the crowd and we crouched hiding behind one of the giant oak doors.

"My dad told me the story of how all this began."

"What began?" I asked, confused.

"This island and our way of living, with Obeah at the healm…"

"And?"

"Well, there was a native community. Farmers, sailors, and medicine men. All lived off the land much how we do now, but they had no faith. They prayed to the birds, and the weather patterns and the stars for safekeeping on the water, and good crops in the summer and autumn months. When Obeah crash landed here, they'd never seen a plane before–"

"They thought he was something special because of that?"

"Well, not exactly, but it helped his sway over the people. At first he told his stories of *The Sky Ones* as a means to build relationships with the island custodians. They too would share their own stories of healing and magic. Obeah started to counter their beliefs and replace them with his own. He used the plane as proof of the power of *The Sky Ones*. The people we live among now are those that believed Obeah, and supported his governorship – because he brought the radio, and the plane. Back then he left often for things like medicine and grain."

"So what happened to the natives that did not believe?"

"Dad said that he couldn't tell me what happened to the ones that stayed. But most fled."

"But–"

"–Shh, listen. Dad made me swear not to tell a soul. Please do not repeat any of this ever. I am only telling you, because there is a place out there that knows of him. There is a place that cannot be too far beyond our small horizon that could help. I will help you Anwen. We have to try. None of the other children would read what I gave them."

"Come on lets walk before Justin spots us." We snuck out joining the back of the line.

"They are too afraid to do anything. But I'm not. I need to do it for my mum. That's the only reason Dad is weakening in his faith. How can a man that claims to care for all of us abandon my mother like this?"

"Everything okay you two?" Came Justin's harsh voice.

101

I gasped. He was right behind us. We hadn't even noticed him join the line.

"Course, just talking about the flag repairs Mum and I will be doing." I smiled as Justin walked by us. He held his eyes on mine until I turned away to walk Egret to her door.

"Perhaps the flag setting fire a sign from the Sky Ones?" Egret shouted to him over her shoulder.

"What do you know?" Snapped Justin as he followed closely behind us. Stopping only as we crossed the threshold ino Egret's garden.

Mum had brought the great flag home and laid it out across the entire living room floor.

"We'll clean it first." She smiled. Pleased to have a joint venture again. I nodded in agreement.

"I'm a little tired now though, could we do it tomorrow?" I asked yawning.

"Of course my little minnow." It was a pet name I hadn't heard since the day Dad had congratulated me on holding my breath for three minutes. It almost choked me to hear it now. I hadn't practiced in so long. I climbed into bed for the night while Mum continued to clean up down stairs. She was humming again. My heart ached at the memory of us back on Shelagh, when climbing and swinging, and swimming was a daily occurrence. I lay there holding my breath until my lungs kicked out at my chest. Counting. And then I admitted it to myself, no other idea would replace it. The flag would be my parachute to the boat. I had a plan. I had a plan in place. Now all I needed to do was gather my army- if there was such a thing.

13

Chapter 13

It was the 21st of December. The winter solstice. The longest night of the year in the northern hemisphere. The island was due to fall into darkness at 3:35pm. The sun wouldn't rise again until nearly 9:00am the next day. It was freezing now. Mum and I were back in our big rain macs and wool jumpers that we had arrived in. There were no celebrations as such, not like those in my book on the pagans – they would have huge fire festivals and dance into the night in celebration of the returning light. Obeah did however, let school out for the day. His logic was that children could help their families gather firewood for the coming week of rest. A week of hibernation Mum had explained to me. I wanted to make the most of the free time away from prying eyes, so I offered to go out collecting firewood by myself. I thought it might be the last time I could release a message on a paper bird before my attempt at escape. The island was readying to get sleepier than ever.

"You're trusting her to go out alone yet again?" Obeah had hissed at my mum when he'd visited the house that morning.

Having heard about the note past to Thomas, Obeah was getting ever more paranoid about the children of the island. He was starting to develop a sort of tick, constantly looking about him as if he were afraid of some shadow at his shoulder.

"It's for firewood Obeah, she has been so good lately don't you think?"

"I think the woods is where all the trouble starts." He almost sneered then, losing his air of control because Mum offered him an opinion of her own.

"Well, I think it will be good for Anwen to have some time to herself. It is almost Christmas after all."

"There is no Christmas here." Obeah shouted pointing his index finger right into the tip of Mum's nose. She was shocked, her mouth dropped open, speechless. This man had pretended to be a great friend, and now he was treating her like a dog. Mum smoothed out her apron and cleared her throat.

"Well then—"

"You will join the outlanders up in the fields if you blaspheme like that again on my island."

"I thought you cared for those people up there Obeah. Why do you keep using their way of life as a threat?" She was gentle with her words. I could see she was getting more and more nervous around him. He was becoming more and more unpredictable – unravelling.

"I will say what I like, and you will stop questioning." His voice was a deeper lower rumble than he'd ever used in our presence. Like tectonic plates starting to shift and ready for an earth shattering moment. Neither of them had seen me watching from the ladder. I waited for a few moments after Obeah had left. Then I came rushing down as if nothing had happened.

"I won't be long, and I'll be on my best behaviour. Promise."
I kissed Mum on the cheek, which I hadn't done in so long.
She remained still and silent. Stunned. I left in my feigned
ignorance, but inside fury burned brighter than ever. The
beast had now turned on my mother.

I went to the bay where we had arrived all those months ago.
Summer had barely seemed to happen. One thing I noticed as
missing straight away, was the bird song. It was like all that
life had disappeared. The sky was white and listless without a
cloud to tell a story. I missed the warmth of the southern seas
so much. It was also the bay where Egret and I had found Dad's
radio and learned of Obeah's great deceit. I walked along the
line of trees that faced the horizon, looking out to where Dad
lived somewhere- alone, without us. I felt certain he was still
alive. I kicked up sand, walked and sulked, suddenly overtaken
by such a deep sadness. It was almost Christmas as I knew
it – a time of celebration, indulgence and friends. But there
would be no Christmas here. When I had told Egret about
barbecues on the beach and presents from Saint Nick, she had
never even heard of such a thing. I half-heartedly picked up any
dry looking sticks for kindling. Mum had given me a foraging
basket which I had slung across my body with its leather strap.
The whole basket was almost as big as my torso. But the yellow
rain Mac and thick jumper cushioned me from its harsh wicker.

Something caught my eye then. In the sky up ahead. It was a
huge bird heading directly towards me. It was getting closer,
lower and bigger. It's wing span seemed to be wider than I was
tall. Once it was within a few hundred meters, I realised it was a
sea eagle; huge and majestic, it's mottled brown wings sparked
with the yellows of the absent sun. Its head held high and breast
strong. I stopped still at the shoreline awaiting its landing,

trusting it wouldn't hit, but trying hard not to flinch anyway. It wore a leather blinder over its head – a sort of blindfold that the bird seemed to be okay with. It was a burgundy red leather with small green feathers stood on top. It was a falconer's bird, and I realised we had met before. It was a bird that belonged to the princess of Nelawi; The pirate like woman I had loved so much. For a split second I wondered whether I should make a run for it – so menacing was its size as it flung back its wings and set forward its talons ready to land. I remembered his name as Marmaduke. It suited him. I took a step backward as the bird landed before me, he had a small scroll rolled up and tucked into the buckle of the blinder. We stood still a moment, taking each other in.

"Can I?" I asked gently, stepping carefully toward him. He remained steadfast and simply turned his head to look away from me as I approached. As though I were far to lowly to acknowledge. I liked him. He was only a foot shorter than me. He could have bowled me over with ease. His wings were smooth and muscular looking. Their waxy browns and golds reflecting the low winter sunlight that was trying hard to pierce through thick cloud. I crouched low and tentatively reached for the scroll. I was as gentle as I could be and it slid out of its case easily. I unrolled it and read the words with such a hunger that they didn't fully register first time round, so I took a breath and read it again;

We have received your message and we are coming. Approaching from the south
of the island in a few days. We know your position and believe you and
your family to be in grave danger.

106

Princess Nebatu

Those words were like heaven to my mind. A giggle burst out of me, my body fizzed and thrummed. I stood there for a long time reading and re-reading the note. The sea eagle turned its head to face me after a long few moments. When I looked up at him once more I said

"Thank you." This was his cue to leave. The beautiful creature spread his wings to their fullest potential, as wide as he was tall. I knew instinctively to take another step back. His wings batted backward, his legs bent, and with one powerful jump he lifted off and was gone. I watched the bird as he re-joined the wind, wings wide open.

She was coming. Princess Nebatu of Nelawi had found me. By some miracle. Now I had an army. I couldn't wait a day longer. Help was coming, and this gave me the last ounce of courage I needed to go ahead with my escape plan. I would go and meet the Princess before they arrived. I could give them valuable information about the island that would ensure our success. It was time to action my escape plans. I needed to get to Egret and fast. I ran up the beach and through the opening of the trees as quickly as I could. The sand was slipping from beneath me, slowing me. I panted hard and pushed on until the sand turned to the mud of the forest floor. As I exited the trees into the centre of the village, I slowed my pace and stopped to catch my breath. I didn't want to rouse suspicion. As I entered the clearing, I could see Egret straight away. She was tending to her garden. Probably picking potatoes I had thought. She was kneeling with her back to me. I approached her and tapped her on the shoulder. She turned to look up at me and I could see at once that she had been crying. Her eyes were red rimmed and glassy. She sniffed when she saw me and stood to face me.

"Egret. What's the matter?" She sniffed and wiped her nose on the sleeve of her grey woollen coat.

"It's mother, she, she-" Egret choked on the words gasping a sob back into her, as if trying to pull backward through time. I knew already before she spoke. I wrapped my arms around her and held her tight.

"She's gone." Egret's whole body shook as the sobs took over her. We held each other there in her rectangular front garden for a long time. I just let my best friend cry there on my shoulder; sniffing and hiccuping until there was nothing left. When she went quiet, I held her at arm's length and spoke.

"I have to go tonight, Egret. People are coming. Someone is coming to help. They are just days away, but I can't wait a moment longer. Something strange is in the air...I-"

"It's okay Anwen. I understand. You know Thomas agreed to run with us?" She looked to the floor and my heart ached. I felt like I was betraying her in her moment of need, but the pull to act was too strong. As the sky turned the deep indigo of dusk and the air began to crisp and mist up with every breath. I just knew that this cloudless night was calling me 'now or never'.

"Then he can take your place. We'll be back in a few days. It's the princess of Nelawi coming. I just knew there was some link to Nelawi here– in Obeah's stolen faith about Kunda and Beacrow. A sea eagle came with the message. It feels like fate Egret. I can't ignore it. I will fetch Thomas. But I know you need to stay and take care of your dad." She looked up at me then, her wild auburn curls brushed across her face in the icy evening breeze. Her face was mostly in shadow, lit only by the light filtering out through her front window. I felt some relief at not being able to see her full disappointment in me. She nodded and then her father called from the house.

"Egret where are you?" I could hear the falter in his voice. She hugged me tight and said,

"Good luck Anwen." She turned and ran back into the house.

Thomas had been the only other person in the classroom that had responded to one of our notes, and he'd quietly taken the punishment for owning one. He could have betrayed me over and over having also caught me coming down from the outlanders. Yet he had never said a thing. I knew without doubt I could trust in him.

As awful as this is to admit, the news of Egret's mother passing did give me a legitimate reason to knock at Thomas' house. No one here ever seemed to interact after tea time. It was out of the ordinary to receive a knock at the door, but I had good reason now. I needed to get Thomas out of there. There was no way I could do this alone.

Thomas was strong despite his lanky stance, I had seen him hauling heavy loads for his gran during harvest, and his sign language meant that he would be able to communicate with me across distances without fear of us being heard.

I found Thomas' front door easily enough. His was the house in the very centre of the row. There were five houses to the left of it, and five to the right of it. His was the in between place, right in the middle . He lived with his grandma, who he described as 'quiet but deadly' which made me laugh – to think of a frail old woman being scary in any way. But Thomas assured me she ruled harshly and never let him skip a chore. 'If I even miss something out of forgetfulness, it's the wooden spoon at the back of the knees.' He had assured Egret and I. We both winced at the thought of the wooden spoon. Thomas' grandma had known the island before the arrival of Obeah, but

109

Thomas was not allowed to talk about it. No matter how I had prodded for more, his fear was too great to break his promise to his gran. I knocked on his front door as loud as I could. My palms started to sweat at the thought of meeting the harsh old woman. My tongue felt heavy and dry in my mouth. I only realised I had been holding my breath when Thomas answered, and I physically sighed. My shoulders relaxing at the same time. The light of the day was fading fast, and the air started to have a frosty bite.

"Bad news-"

"What?" his face contorted in concern. I spoke, probably louder than I needed to in hope that his gran might hear and leave us be.

"Anwen's mother has passed away." Thomas stood in silence. Blank faced for a good few moments, until a frail voice rode out on the mild night time breeze

"Who's there?"

"Hang on." He said to me and disappeared for a long moment shutting the door behind him.

When he came back, he was wrapping his grey winter coat over his shoulders and shut the door behind him.

"Come on-" He said walking out in front of me and leading the way. I secretly made him my hero in that moment "Let's go see her." I followed him quickening my pace to keep with his step.

"Thomas wait. There's something else."

I went on to explain to him, all the reasons why the escape plan had to be tonight. I told him about the sea eagle and the falconer Princess Nebatu, who was coming to our aid. I couldn't fully explain to myself why it felt so urgent to get to them before they got to us. I somehow felt on a back foot otherwise. As if Obeah might intercept them before they got to us. I really did not want that to happen, this felt like our last chance.

"I'm coming with you." Thomas announced with a proud chest, and I wanted to hug him so bad-but Thomas was not a hugger. I had once wrapped an arm over his shoulder, and he just recoiled from me so taken aback by the affection. So when he told me he was coming I tried to keep cool and just said,

"Great."

"But we have to go and see Egret first. I want to give her my condolences and check she's okay about us leaving without her. It's not a good omen to leave a friend behind." His eyes were sad as he spoke. There was a quiet bond between the children here. It went way beyond my few months on the island.

"You're right. Come on." We walked quickly down the pathway back to Egret's house. She was sitting out on her doorstep as if she were expecting us. She was wearing her grey coat still, and she had a knapsack strapped over both shoulders. On seeing us she stood and ran to meet us. She blocked our way at the foot of her garden path. The vegetable patch made it too narrow for more than one person.

"Come on." She said barging passed us both and walking toward Obeah's back garden. Towards where Mum and I were staying in the cabin. Where we now needed to remove the flag without being seen. It was in the loft bedroom, sewn and retied ready to return to its rightful place atop the silver birch flagpole. I had left the trap door to the roof unlatched so that I could climb in and steal it.

"Egret?" Thomas called after her.

"Shhh." She snapped over her shoulder. We both caught up with her and matched her pace. Both of them were a foot taller than me. I was getting breathless trying to keep up. Once we were walking in a row she whispered loudly as we kept walking.

"I'm coming. I've told Dad everything. He's going to cover for us and tell the islanders that you are both staying with us. He will tell them that I am in despair and won't leave my room. You two are my only two close friends. Tom, Dad will tell your gran that you are reciting the Book of Sky to me every day – that should put her off for a bit." Thomas snorted then.

"She will love that-" Thomas smiled. Then a fear hit me.

"But now you've told your *dad* Egret." I was panicking.

"How do you know your dad won't try and stop us? Or change his mind and tell Obeah?" I ranted at her, my best friend who had just lost her mother.

"Anwen. It's okay. I promise. Dad is furious. And sad. He said we should have got Mum help, we should be allowed to leave the island. We're all prisoners here. Compliant prisoners. And what for?" Egret's dad was a quiet man. Tall and thin, frail almost. But his eyes glistened. I remembered him from our first day arriving at the worship space. He wore the black and white like everyone else. But he didn't flock around Obeah like all the others. They were all like metal to a magnet. But he stayed aside and watched on. I'd never got to meet Egret's mother.

"Okay. I trust you." I said grabbing her hand and squeezing. We'd stopped naturally to listen to one another speak, but then something – someone blocked our path. Justin.

"And where do you think you're going? It's solstice."

"Egret's mother has passed on." I snapped automatically and immediately felt awful for using my friend's mother as our excuse to pass this bully boy. His face did soften, his eyes widened at the news. He looked like he might offer a 'sorry', like he might have some human emotion in there somewhere.

"Well you still shouldn't be here. Why are you heading towards Obeah's house?"

"Well doesn't he mark the dead?" I snapped, and then chipped in

"Plus, I live there too remember? In his lodge." He narrowed his eyes on me. The contempt was mutual.

"I know what you're up to, the three of you. You think a bunch of children can challenge Uncle's power. You're insane." He hissed.

"Oh we know Justin. We wouldn't dream of it." I nodded solemnly.

"It doesn't matter. I'm watching and you won't get away with it. You and your annoying mother will be gone soon anyway. Just three days until sacrifice." He spat the words at me, because they were intended to hurt. They were intended to create fear, ultimately like everything else here. Something inside me cracked at the recognition of what those words meant. The last piece of that puzzle.

"What?" I retorted.

"Don't you remember, Egret and Thomas?" He laughed coldly then, his features were haunting in the shadows of the night. His white hair made him ghost like.

"Of course you don't. None of you do, do you? It's only Mum, Obeah and I that have the capacity to know the truth." Egret and Thomas looked at one another, dumbfounded. Both their expressions were blank and searching. Like they held the thing in their mind but couldn't grasp it, a butterfly fluttering, too quick to be caught in the net.

"What he's talking about?" I pressed them to remember. The three of us stood there like the last of the tenpins waiting to be bowled over. Justin was enjoying being the deliverer of the blow.

"Last in first out. You didn't actually think Obeah was falling for your mum, did you?" He laughed again. "What? You thought you'd be the governor's stepdaughter? You know, you both turned up just in time. In fact, you might even be saving Egret's skin. You see, in order for Obeah to keep his power and peace with Kunda, he must deliver her two human lives every year. One just after each of the solstices. We're a close knit bunch here. We like to protect our own if we can."

"You're lying." I shouted louder than I'd intended. I pushed him with the full force of my body. Explosive. He let me. He knew he had the one up. He stumbled backward but remained standing.

"It's true." Cut in Egret, her face solemn and pale in her remembering. This island did strange things to people- the wine, and the chants, and the manipulation distorted things. It blurred people's minds.

"How did we not remember Thomas?" Thomas remained quiet. Then Justin barged my shoulder passing by. Satisfied he'd defeated us with his words.

"Good luck in getting away by Wednesday. I dare you to take to the sea in this cold." But Justin had no idea what I had up my sleeve. And he had no idea how good I was at being cold.

"Come on." I said, trying not to think about the horror of human sacrifice, or what that might look like, or how Mum's life was at risk if I left and failed, and never returned. Yes, I tried really, really hard not to think about any of those things.

"What's the plan?" Asked Egret. As she and Thomas now struggled to keep up with me.

"We get the flag as quickly as we can and get up the hill over the western cliffs as quickly as we can. I have rope already packed in my bag. I'll climb the oak tree, I'll need your help to winch the fabric up to me. Then you two head straight to the East Bay. The wind is blowing from the west tonight. And there are no clouds, so the night is on our side. The flag is going to be my parachute-"

"-Wait what?" Egret grabbed both of our arms and halted us.

"Anwen that is insane. That will never work. You could die." Egret pleaded with me.

"I agree." Thomas added with a hard nod.

"Look..." I went on, desperate to get them on side. I believed in the plan and it was the only one I had. "...A parachute works by the force of air hitting the fabric in all the right places. Creating a sort of giant wing. Obeah thinks I've been fixing the flag, but I've been sewing lightweight ropes at intervals across the canvass that will act like my steering – just like a real parachute. The flag will be controlled by pulling down on my home-made steering lines which will change the shape of the wing, cause it to turn, or to increase or decrease its rate of descent-"

"-Whoah. Where did that come from?" Thomas nodded his head impressed. I shrugged it off.

"Lord Parkinson of Betaland. He's like the coolest man on earth, and he parachutes to his quarters every day, he taught me all about it in song form- which makes it really easy to remember. So, as I was saying. If I land close enough to the boat, I am sure I could sail her round to you in about 45 minutes. You guys will wait within the trees. Where we found the radio, Egret?"

"Anwen, are you sure about this? It all seems so dangerous. I don't know if we are the right people for the job, are we

Thomas?" She nibbled on her thumb nail.

"Egret." Thomas turned and held her by the shoulders "You are one of the bravest people I have ever met. I know I haven't met many people – but you are one of the bravest. You barely even flinch at the cane, and you never cower to Justin in the same way I see others do all the time. Anwen is an ocean explorer and you are my warrior friend. We can definitely do this." Egret nodded trying to believe in his words.

"Okay." She said "Let's get going. Carry on Anwen." We continued to walk into the darkness finding our way to the back of the lodge that had been my home these past months. I was whispering now.

"We'll need to head south which is where the princess will be sailing from. I have three candles in my backpack and one box of matches. When you see any kind of flame within 100 metres start heading towards me. It will take a while to get the boat out of the bay and over any clashes in current as we head out to sea." I surprised myself. I sounded just like my dad.

"I will sail in as close to the beach as I can, but you may need to wade out to me okay?"

"Okay." Both answered in chorus.

"But first we need to get that flag. Thomas, I will need you to distract my mum while I climb up into our room to get the flag down. Egret can you stay on guard below?" Egret nodded. "If you knock on the door, you can tell Mum about Egret's mother passing, sorry Egret-"

"It's fine." She shook her head and waved away my apology. "She would want this. She asked Dad to leave so many times." I rubbed her shoulder.

"I'm so sorry… Thomas, if you tell Mum, you can then set out that we are all staying with Egret for a couple of nights. If she asks about permission from Obeah, just say it's been granted. By the time anyone notices we're gone it will be too late for them to find us." One final nod from Egret and Thomas and the deal was sealed. The escape was on.

I opened the trap door to our bedroom at the precise moment I heard Mum open the door to Thomas. The flag was already folded up as compact as possible and tied up tight. It would still be like carrying a small child under my arm. I could hear the muffled conversation going on below. I lowered gently onto our rainbow blanket bed and slid to the floor. I lifted the flag and pushed it up out of the trap door first. Then I climbed back up and out onto the roof. I peered back in through the open hatch and caught Thomas' eye across the room. I gave him a thumbs up. He looked back to Mum, and she looked over her shoulder to where his eyes had drifted. I froze and held my breath.

"Sure!" Thomas raised his voice to pull her attention back again. She looked straight at him. He cleared his throat.

"Sure Ms Laura, I, I will tell her. We will drop by tomorrow for the soup. Sleep well now. See you."

"Thank you Thomas." And as Mum closed the door, slowly, suspiciously. I carefully, closed the rooftop trap door.

The flag was heavy, but we made it up to the oak tree at westerly point unseen. The Hill was steep, and we were all breathless. Our exhales rose to the stars like smoke.

"Look." I pointed upward.

"There's Orion that's the constellation we'll be following tonight."

Orion is the only constellation you can rely on wherever you are and at whatever time of night. As the earth moves and turns, the stars move too, but weirdly Orion appears to remain a still point in the sky – not even the north star can do this for a man, or in my case, a girl trying to navigate the wild wide open ocean.

It was all going to plan. I had made it to the top of the tree, the flag on my lap. My heart pounded hard in my chest, my cheeks felt hot while the air was like ice. My adrenaline had begun to kick in, and I was sweating and freezing all at the same time. But I was ready, no going back. Thomas and Egret had managed to hook the rope over the branch where I sat. From there, with their help, I was able to haul the flag – or should I say, my parachute, up into the tree. I was crouching low on the branch to keep my balance. I carefully began unravelling the outer rope, the flag was otherwise folded in the perfect way to open up on the wind, just like origami. Just as if it were neatly set up inside a knapsack. It was still a worrying job to untie it – but it was my only practical choice in getting to Obeah's sail boat safely. The leaves had long fallen from the trees, so I had a good view out to sea. I was at the highest possible point I was able to reach. I snapped off any small snagging branches that surrounded me, and might risk the integrity of the fabric. I strapped the parachute to my arms, being careful to keep the pieces of rope separate from one another. Beyond that it would be a leap of faith.

"Okay, I'm ready." I shouted as my two friends watched on in great trepidation.

I waited in the high branches of the oak tree until the wind picked up. And then whoosh I jumped, releasing my flag-parachute up overhead. I was flying. The wind was biting cold, but I couldn't stifle a wide smile. Tears were blown onto my cheeks. I held onto those ropes for dear life. For it really was life or death now, and my body knew it. My pulse thumped hard and fast in my ears. Every other smell and sound was heightened. Like I was some animal being hunted. I could smell the salt of the sea and the sweetness of decaying apples long fallen and buried beneath leaves of brown and orange. I could hear the rush of wind that I now relied upon to keep my parachute afloat. Every ruffle and scrape seemed to echo like it was all happening in my head. The trees below were silhouetted in the moonlight, their bare branches warning me not to fail, or else. It was a brief crossing of that treacherous terrain, and then I was above the welcoming glint of sea bedazzled in starlight. It felt like the stars were cheering me on, winking at me- proud of my courage to join them in the sky. Before I knew it, I was descending. Like a sycamore seed floating down with the wind cushioning its release. Down. Down. Down. And into the water with such an exhilarating splash. It was ice cold, every fibre of my skin prickled. I loved it. The landing was like a slap back to reality. I released the flag-parachute into the gentle waves. Its fabric spread out onto the waters surface and left to the will of the sea. I spun looking for the sailboat. In my stupor, I'd flown too far. The boat was behind me and closer to the cliffs than I had expected.

"Damn." I had to swim back towards the island to get to it. I felt heavy in my clothes, like they were the anchor and chain, I tugged, pulled and paddled desperately against them. But I eventually made it to the boat- slower than I would have liked, but alive.

Once I was in the boat shivering kicked in. My teeth chattered, and I gritted them tight to try and keep control over my senses. Joanie, the outlander had been right, it was a small boat. We wouldn't have fit any more than three of us inside. It was like the boat my dad had used to teach me to sail when

I was five – recreational, definitely no Shelagh. My frozen fingers fumbled at the ropes, my muscles felt like lead. I needed to get out of my wet clothes but my spares were with Egret. I had to hold it together until I reached my friends. I fought against thoughts that told me this was never going to work. I hoisted and pulled. The sails went up, and all of a sudden the wind died down.

"No. No, no, no, no, no, nooooo." My eyes went searching the deck. There were oars. I started to untie them only to realise I'd never make it rowing. I pulled at a cushion over the back bench – it was hinged. I lifted the top to discover that yes, there was an engine.

"Thank God." I slapped my hands together in prayer-something I had never done in my life, yet it came so naturally in my desperate moment. I tugged at the choke lever once – a light rumble and then nothing. Twice, a slightly bigger rumble that coughed and spluttered back to nothing.

"Please. Please? Please?" I pulled, and pulled, and pulled and then-ignition. The Vrrooom vrrroooom of power. I pulled at the main sail and we were away.

"Wahhooooh!" The wind was slowly freezing my face, but I was on my way. The clouds had shifted, and the night was now lit perfectly by the waxing moon. As I turned the corner towards the beach where Thomas and Egret were waiting, I tried to light my candles to signal them to come. Of course, my soaked clothes dripped all over the match box and my fingers had lost all dexterity. There was no way the candles would light. But I could see the silhouette of their figures stood upon the white sand waiting. I waved my arms with all I had left, and they waved back. Thomas gave a thumbs up and a thumbs down signal to me, holding his hand high for me to see. It was a question. I gave him a thumbs up in return and beckoned them towards me as I could feel the hull nudging its way into the sand bar. They waded in, but I was still too far out. Both Thomas and Egret held a knapsack above their heads. These bags held clothes, water and canned food taken from their emergency pantries. It was imperative that we save them.

"It's too deep Anwen, we'll be in at our waists and then we'll freeze. There's only two sets of spare clothes. If you don't change quick you're done for." Egret was fretting, I could see her looking back at the beach, the call of safety, the call of the predictable.

"Egret." I called her attention back to me- "It will be fine, look-" I looked about me trying to think quick, and in that moment, where all the pressure combusted within me to get this right, an idea came –"Look, I'm already soaked through and I'm basically a mermaid at holding my breath. Throw me the bags and I will jump in and take you on my shoulders."

"You will never carry me." Thomas shook his head laughing.

"Yes I will, I held my dad for like one second once, so that definitely equals ten seconds for you Thomas."

"Anwen?" Thomas tried to protest.

"Thomas, please. We don't have much time just throw me your bag." And he did.

"Egret? Throw me yours." And she did. And then with the shivers already threatening to swallow me whole, I dived back into the bone biting cold of my saltwater home, and I swam to them. Egret first. I got to hands and knees to load her onto my shoulders and stood, and walked. It was like wading through clay, and then after a few metres I was submerged. I took the biggest gulp I could before my head went beneath the surface. Egret held her legs up out of the water. I gripped her knees for dear life to keep balance. Otherwise my world was an inky black, frozen nothingness. Each step felt like lifting feet of steel. A moment passed, and my lungs thumped at my diaphragm to gasp at air that wasn't there. I heard her scream something from above me, and suddenly her weight was pulled from me. I swam up, gasping and coughing, sucking at the cold solstice air. We'd made it to the boat. I looked back for Thomas, holding the side of the boat to gather my senses. He was gone.

"Thomas!" I shouted, but my voice couldn't carry. Then Egret shouted above me.

"Thomas!"

"Did Justin follow us?" I looked up at Egret who was now safely inside the boat.

And then a shadow beneath us. Thomas burst through the surface right in front of me.

"Thomas." I yelled "You nearly killed me. I thought you couldn't swim."

"I can't, I just kicked my legs and hoped. Come on, let's put those spare clothes to good use." He climbed into the boat and pulled me up, my strength now completely gone. Thomas looked away while Egret helped me to change. We were a mess of bad ideas, but we were together and in the boat. We sat on the back bench and huddled in close. We were ready to set sail in search of Princess Nebatu.

14

Chapter 14

D ad used to tell me stories about all the different religions of the world. He told me how he thought that lots of the stories he'd been told sounded very similar. Like the story of the Celtic goddess Brigid and the Hindu Goddess Saraswati. Both females and both said to have the magic to share the gift of creativity and wisdom with those that worship them.

Saraswati's story goes like this; She rides the rivers upon a great swan sharing the beauty of music, wisdom and words. She is protector and inspirer of all things creative and life giving.

And Brigid's story goes like this; Goddess of the Celtic lands, she is the mother of the bards, the sharer and creator of all earth's beautiful secrets. Both goddesses shared in their desire to protect and create. They seemed like a sisterhood to me.

Dad always said that he didn't care what people believed. We are all the same at our core. I tried to believe the same. Dad never really believed that there were any magical beings in the sky, or that prayers could bring better luck to worshippers than non-believers. Even so, I prayed every moment that we sailed into the night. I prayed for Mum's safety. I prayed we wouldn't die. I prayed that the wind and the engine would bring us into the pathway of the princess, and then the sun began to rise. The sky was cold but ablaze like fire. Reds and oranges welcomed us towards the horizon. A pathway of golden sparkles reflected the sun's light as gentle wind waves lapped across the waters surface. It was as though they were twinkling, beckoning us on. The three of us all sat squeezing in against one another for warmth. There was no land in sight. Just sea and sky for an eternity. A scene that had once been my heaven, suddenly filled me with panic. The sunrise helped me to reset our course towards south. The wind having veered us slightly to the east.

"Thank God, we have you." Said Thomas. He was looking a little worried now too.

"Yes, when all this is over. I want you to teach me how to sail." Smiled Egret. We'd passed the long cold night by telling each other stories about any memories we could find beyond Obeah and the island. We were all surprised to find that our stories were fading, hard to grasp at like dandelion seeds drifting away on the wind. The sky was getting brighter, painted with wisps of purple and blue, the sea glittered under the soft light of dawn. It was calm and still as though the world were holding its breath for us.

"We might not have that much longer to wait." Shouted Thomas as he stood excitedly pointing in the distance. There was a giant merchant vessel with a gold mermaid mounted on its helm. A crowd of people lined up behind her, a sea eagle circled above it. Dragon like. One woman hung high from the main mast standing out from all the rest of the crew. A mass of chocolatey curls flailing all about her head, a red-kite sat proud upon her shoulder. It was her – Princess Nebatu.

124

We were hoisted up on the old white life raft. To me, they are just rubber rings, but Dad always assured me they were a bit tougher than that. The welcome we received made it feel as though we'd known everyone for a hundred years. The crew clapped and whooped and patted our shoulders. Some of them pulled us in for a hug. There were at least thirty of them; an equal mix of men and women. All of them wore their hair long, with plaits weaved within their messy locks. Their clothes were all animal skins and hides. They looked how I imagined the Vikings would have looked all those eons ago. Princess Nebatu greeted us with just as warm a welcome. She too had plaits braided in among her wild curls. Her plaits however, had pearls and small gems woven within them. Her face was weathered by the sun and the sea, but her eyes were soft and kind; they were the blue- green of shallow ocean, crystal-like allowing you to see right into her soul. Just as crystal clear waters let you see the rocks and dangers that lay beneath it. The princess herself was anything but shallow. She seemed to be able to communicate with the birds by a simple look or a nod. It was as though they had their own secret language that no one else was privy to.

We were invited below deck where there was a huge open space filled with a giant oak table in the shape of an octagon. Eight edges for eight members of the crew to stand and talk strategy. I felt like a pirate now. Luca, the head skipper made space for the three of us next to him. Then the princess gave a brief introduction to everyone. It was impossible to remember them all, but Luca and Francesca stood out. The two stood together, taller than the rest. Francesca was completely bald, her face decorated in blue-green paints, her eyelids painted silver. Luca wore an armoured vest adorned with symbols that indicated his status within the army. Princess Nebatu, Luca and Francesca were the key players in the battle yet to come.

"Ladies and gentlemen, this is the daughter of great celestial cartographer Guy Mcqueen. Sadly, Mcqueen is currently missing. He never made it to his appointment in Europa." She turned to me then, I was opposite her at the table.

"Anwen, I assure you that I have set my best seafarers to the task of locating your father. We have narrowed down an area where we think he may have hit trouble. Meanwhile, your messages reached our shores – like magic." She smiled and winked then, and the red kite on her shoulder squawked in agreement with her. The sea eagle was perched on the branch of an olive tree in the far corner. The tree stood in a huge clay pot positioned directly under the slice of sunlight that poured down through the hatch opening. The bird was huge. His head nodded once at the word 'magic' too.

"We, the people of Nelawi have known about this island for a long time, but no one has ever been able to locate it. Every time we think we know where to find it, it's as if it shifts and morphs. But with your messages we were able to track the winds and tides back to you. How did you find us?" She asked with a sly smile as if she already knew.

"I just figured heading south was my only reasonable option." I shrugged.

"Of course." She nodded in a sign of respect.

"And you two? Are you islanders?" Speechless, gormless almost, Egret and Thomas nodded. Both looking very formal in their matching grey wool coats.

"I am sorry for you. Although you probably have no idea of the dangers that you have all been exposed to over the last decade." She nodded to the head skipper Luca then and he picked up the story from there.

"Obeah was one of us; a Nelawiti. Our tribes are like family. We stick together and we base our kinship on loyalty and trust." His voice was deep and soothing like a cello. He was a giant of a man, broad and wide with dark brooding eyes, though there was a softness that made me feel at ease in his company. He went on.

"Obeah was trusted on a mission to find this island. Kunda is a force of great healing power. She is the snake of life coiled up in the heart of the island, goddess of the northern seas. Our ancestors knew that just one drop of her venom could save many lives. We wanted to find her so that we could cure our people from an outbreak of disease that spread aggressively through our country. Obeah sent message that he'd found the island, but then we lost all contact. He had become corrupted in wanting the antidote all to himself." It was the final piece of the puzzle.

"But what's the point in him keeping it all to himself? No one on the island knows of this..." I reached for Egret's hand "...Egret's mother has just passed away. Obeah would not let them leave the island for help, nor did he offer anything like medicine to her. He won't let the islanders swim or play. It's like a black and white world." Egret bowed her head, and I squeezed her hand a little tighter. The princess spoke then-

"Totalitarian power can do a lot for a bruised ego. Obeah had always wanted to be head of my army, but unfortunately, his skills could never match those of Luca here." She nodded to Luca and he spoke again-

"Obeah was always a fearful man. Power and fear make for a very dangerous mix. He *was* however, one of only three pilots in our territory and he took our only plane. Many people lost their lives when we could not get them to medical facilities with the speed of that plane." Luca looked to the floor then, and Princess Nebatu picked up where he left off

"That includes Luca's father. He was head of our army before Luca, but he died of pneumonia. Our lands are vast and dessertous as you may remember." I nodded.

"If Obeah has harnessed Kunda's power and learned how to control his people, then no amount of fighting will bring us any victory. We need to capture him." The princess finished and then nodded to Francesca. Francesca was the only person with no hair at all, her head was shaved tight to her skull and she had spiral tattoos above each of her ears – a symbol for rebirth and eternity.

"I was one of the original tribes' people on Sedna Island. My people shared the fish stocks of the island's waters with the Goddess Kunda, or she shared them with us. We never over fished, we took only what we needed. We would offer those that had died of natural causes to the Goddess for consumption and rebirth. Perhaps that was the start of her hunger for humans. When Obeah came, he started manipulating and dividing the people. He claimed he was sent by the one True God *The Sky One Beacrow-*"

"-Beacrow is the God of the southern skies. We prayed for him to fly beside Obeah to keep him safe and return him to us in triumph. But our skies have been empty of magic ever since." Said the princess sadly. Francesca continued speaking

"Some people believed Obeah, that he was the chosen one and that Kunda had done something awful to anger Beacrow. But many people didn't believe. A civil war broke out. Obeah trapped the Goddess in the caves below the island and starved her. This caused an earthquake. He learned to appease her with a small amount of food – the people he chose for sacrifice. And he prayed to Beacrow to fix the broken lands. He has manipulated the Gods and the islanders. Many people were offered as sacrifice to Kunda and the rest of us fled. We took all the boats but one. That one boat, the one you have sailed here upon, was left for the next person brave enough to escape Obeah's rule."

"If he controls Kunda and all that healing venom, why doesn't he share it, or trade it? He could have become a rich man." I asked. The princess explained

"That man is an alchemist, he would offer tinctures to our people on Nelawi, but he always had a professor watching over him, someone to answer to. But his knowledge? Well he could always have used that for good or bad. It seems he has kept that magic all to himself – perhaps it's what he feeds to the islanders to keep them on his side, who knows." She shrugged.

"The wine." I said then – the final piece. "At every one of his sermons he feeds the islanders wine. He has rows and rows of fruits trees, and strawberry plants. The strawberries – when I ate them I fainted. When I woke up in his house I was paralysed. He never shared that fruit with anyone, but the wine – he made that all alone and the adults drank it every day. And your ears Thomas, you said he poured the wine in your ears to cure you when you couldn't hear."

"Of course." Agreed Egret. "When we ate the apples that day, under the trees, I felt like I couldn't remember how I'd got them. No one can remember things clearly on the island. It's like there was nothing before him." Thomas rubbed his head trying to absorb everything.

"It is our sworn oath to Francesca to return the island to her as custodian. She holds a true lineage to the land." Said the princess. Then Thomas spoke.

"I think my mother was sacrificed." His brow was scrunched as he tried to grasp at the memory in his mind.

"It's likely. Obeah would definitely know how to blur the memories of people. It was a popular tincture we would create to erase traumatic memories. It's a mix of lilaska, boucca zap and tuwago bark. It is an ancient recipe discovered by our elders. He will have used this to control people if necessary. I feel sure of that now. The fruit garden probably just gave him a luxurious way to disguise it all." The princess looked so hurt to be realising the error of her misplaced trust. Luca walked around the table to her and placed a steady hand upon her bird free shoulder.

"None of this is your fault Princess. He has betrayed everyone."

*

The Princess, Luca and Francesca showed everyone where we were on the map that was rolled out in the centre of the table. Where we were now, and where they expected the island to be. The plan was this; We would approach by night, and we would infiltrate the island. At north, east, south and west, sending a handful of soldiers to each location. Each group would dig a series of traps into the ground, cover them with bamboo and leaves. This is where Thomas, Egret and I came in. We would be the ones to confront Obeah. We would threaten him with the army from Nelawi and then offer to prove it by showing him their merchant's ship at the eastern bay.

Between the three of us, one of us would hopefully antagonise him enough to call him to the bay. It was one of our jobs, whichever one was the most successful in having Obeah follow them, to lead him to the bay via one of the routes where a trap had been set. Each trap would have a sniper, someone hiding out in a tree close by ready to witness and support the capture of the island's governor. Once captured he would be taken to the boat and removed from the island. The princess promised that she would take him back to Nelawi and deal with him according to the law of the land. He would receive a fair trial, and the proper punishment for someone who committed treason. It all seemed pretty simple. And I could feel the adrenaline already buzzing through my veins. I was no longer afraid because I had an army. I had a team, a group of people backing me, behind me, by my side, and ready to fight with me. Ready to rescue me from this place. Ready to help me find my dad and pull my mum away from this awful spell that she had found herself under. It started to take a hold of her from the moment we arrived on the island. We were just a day away from our final escape now.

With an experienced team of seafarers, it was easy enough to find our way back to Sedna Island. In fact, we needed to hold off for a few hours in order to make sure our approach was by night. It was full moon on the 24th of December. Our escape would now have been discovered. We were probably assumed dead. I felt a sudden pang of worry for Mum. I felt sure she would blame herself after all the fighting. Once the traps had been set overnight, Thomas, Egret and I would announce our arrival at sunrise the next day. We would need to manage this carefully and try not to arrouse Obeah too soon.

Thomas, Egret and I each set off with a different group. Thomas going north, Egret joining the group heading west and I stayed with the group remaining in the east. The ground was hard with cold. Trying to dig with spades and forks felt like an impossibility. Progress was slow, and even in the lower temperatures of midwinter I found myself sweating. I could smell the ice and the earth as I tried my hardest to force my spade into the cold hard ground. Each time it felt like I was hitting a rock. It hurt my ankles and reverberated up through my forearms. It felt pointless even trying. At least the men in the group were making some indentations into the ground. We needed each hole to be ten feet deep. It took three hours to dig the first. The second time around Francesca, who was leading my group, had sent somebody back to the ship for pickaxes. This did make the work slightly easier, but not much. Two and a half hours later our second hole was dug about fifty yards from the first, and then a third another fifty yards from the second. Each hole was dug below the right hand side of a particularly characteristic oak tree, so that we'd remember exactly where they were. One had a trunk that appeared split in two; it was two trees wrapping around one another appearing as one. The other two trees were like twins; the same shape and opposite one another, so they were easy to spot if you knew what you were looking for.

We had to assume that the other groups were making similar progress with setting traps in the icy ground. This would make approximately twelve holes in total. Twelve opportunities to capture Obeah. Twelve opportunities to free the people on the island from his rule. And save them from his fictional religion manipulated by himself for himself. We had no means of communication until our meet time at sunrise.

The sky remained clear as dawn began to blanket our little spot on planet Earth. The sky turned from midnight blue to dusky indigo, then to a water wash navy before the pinks, and reds, and oranges of sunrise started to paint itself across the early morning sky. We all sat huddled together in the thicket.

As the sun's position told us it was approximately 7a.m, each member of the group took their position in a tree with a good view of their designated hole. The birds chirped sporadically in the tree tops, as if they were looking out for us, waking up from their winter slumber just to make sure we'd be okay.

It was time for Thomas, Egret and I to meet at the congregation space, where we knew the children of the island would be arriving very soon. We felt no need to announce ourselves, everyone would already know that we were gone by now. It wouldn't take long for everyone to learn that we were back. The shock of it would ripple through the community within just a few moments of our arrival in the centre of the village.

So we waited. Justin was the first to arrive. This meant that Justin, our arch enemy was the first one to notice that we were back. We were safe and alive, we had not only left the island, but we made it back again. Justin's world was about to change forever. It was better than any revenge I could have imagined. The towering congregation space cast a wide shadow out across pathway. Justin squinted to see us. The shock on his face was priceless. His eyes wide and questioning, his jaw to the floor. For once he had no words of fury and hate to pour out. Best of all, he looked afraid – like he'd seen a ghost. The three of us stood proud in front of the thick oak doors of the congregation space. After a long moment of us stood staring at each other. He said nothing at all. He just went running off in the direction of Obeah's house kicking up gravel as he fled. Within a few moments Obeah, Camille and Justin came marching up the short pathway from his grand lodge. They all looked filled with fury, a miniature army. Camille's arms were folded tight across her chest in the cold. The three of them were quickly followed by Thomas's grandma and Egret's father, and then the rest of the community. It didn't occur to me yet that Mum wasn't there. They all made a semi-circle around us, the children staying way back of all the adults. Obeah spoke first.

"You have all broken the rules of the island. I should hold you up in court for treason. And your families. You have brought shame to your families. You've brought shame to me. I am ashamed of you all. I am ashamed to call you Sedna Islanders... And you- You troublemaker..." He pointed a finger at me. A chill of fear rippled through me as his stare felt ice cold upon my skin. I took a step back. He looked unhinged. His usual image of calm and poise had finally unravelled. It was replaced with a fearful, angry dictator about to lose everything.

"...We were a land of peace before you and your traitorous family arrived here. Oh, your mother tried to abide. She tried really hard to be the perfect little devotee. But through you she failed. Who wouldn't fail with a wild thing like you. Thank goodness she is so weak. She's been easier to mould. And you arrived back just in time to see her demise." His lips curled, and Justin smirked looking up at Obeah, desperate to be noticed by him. Almost as if he timed it perfectly. At the very moment he ended that sentence. I heard a shrill scream from inside the congregation space. A shout for help and at once I knew it was Mum.

I spun and pulled at the giant oak doors. Thomas, Egret and I ran inside, quickly followed by the rest of the community. Everyone gave a collective gasp. Mum was tied up to the silver birch flagpole. Her wrists tied above her head, her feet tied at the ankles. It was like being at a witch hunt. In fact, that's exactly what it was. This was always set to be a witch hunt. And it's always the outsider that is targeted. Before us, it had been the outlanders. Members of this society that refused to buy into Obeah's lies. The ones that refused their fate to be governed by lies, sent away to plough the fields until Obeah decided their final destiny. They were the perfect target. A sacrifice. An example to everyone else of what happens to those that disobey, and a feast for a starved Goddess - Kunda. On this occasion, it happened to be Mum.

"Anwen. I'm so sorry." She cried, and sobbed, and sniffed as she spoke. Tied helpless to that sorry tree, the backdrop to Obeah's daily performances.

"Mum." I cried. I ran to her and wrapped my arms around her legs resting my head against her thighs squeezing her tight. I so desperately wished for my dad. She was tied too high for me to reach her hands. I started to fumble with the ropes at her ankles.

"It's no good." She said "It's too late. The ropes are already doused in kerosene. They'll either burn me here alive or take me down to the caves. I hope the rumours aren't true." She sobbed again, her hair loose now and she was in her old dress – the floral one she had worn so often back on Shelagh. All she wanted was to feel that she belonged somewhere. In an odd way I understood it, although I didn't share in her need. I liked my life before. Everyone from the village was there, children and parents. They could all now see the truth of Obeah's reign. Mothers pulled their children close to their chests, afraid to make a mistake in this violent moment. The fathers stood frozen where they were – islands.

"Men." Obeah ordered across the room, "Light the ropes." Four of the nine men, all took the order without question, like dogs they moved towards my mother; the painted mural of heaven and earth the backdrop of her demise. One of the men grabbed me around the waist and pulled me backward, restraining my arms.

"Let go!" I kicked and screamed. The second man knelt and began striking a match. The remaining men joined their families, and they all watched on unsure of what to do, paralysed by the depth of their fear. The sobs of children filled the room singing out a chorus of

"Stop them Daddy please stop them." Then Thomas stepped forward. The first to act-

"Stop!" Everyone turned to look at the tall lanky boy with the floppy dark hair and the signing hands that never stopped dancing. He spoke with authority

"There is an army waiting to strike at the eastern beach." Obeah held up his hand in halt to the man with the match. His eyes fixed on Thomas who was still close to the entrance doors.

"Lies!" Obeah shouted.

"Strike the match Jasaya." Justin shouted in an attempt to meet his uncle's power. The man with the match froze looking from Obeah to Justin. Boy and man turned back to where my mother was tied and away from Thomas.

"I swear it." Thomas raised his right hand in oath, then Egret stood beside him, Obeah and Justin turned to face them again. It was like a chessboard, but no one knew who had check mate.

"It's true. Princess Nebatu, Luca, Francesca and the eagle. They are all here on the island." Egret stated confidently. Obeah took a step forward until he was in a stand-off with my friends.

"How do you know of them? Do not speak of those sinners on my island."

"It's not your island. It never was." I shouted at the top of my lungs. The man holding me squeezed me tighter. I yelled out in pain. The man with the match started to strike it again.

136

"Wait." Obeah held up his hand again.

"Show me." He ordered Thomas and Egret with a sharp lift of his chin. He was used to giving orders now, he no longer tried to feign his character of kind, nurturing leader. His people knew who he was by now. They were still firmly under his spell though. Manipulated and held within his grasp of empty promises and stolen faith. This was it. Thomas and Egret had their chance to lead him through one of their routes and into a trap. They both looked at one another, frozen in fear. One of them needed to take the lead.

"I'll take you." Said Thomas "Egret should be reunited with her father. Go." He nodded to Egret and she went to her father who was stood on the outside of the group of islanders.

"How *sweet of you.*" Obeah praised with a mocking voice. He turned and pointed at the another of his men

"Take the girl and her father to the cellars. They are under arrest for treason. And you-" He turned to face the man with the matches at my mother's feet - the igniter.

"Get her down from there and bring her with us. Make sure both of them-" He pointed at Mum and I "-are tied and bound, then follow us." He turned to me and spoke with measured venom-

"If you make one fowl move, you or *her-*" He pointed at Mum "-Then I will throw you both into the ocean bound as you are. You can drown for all I care, I'll feed your friends to Kunda instead. Not a move out of place."

"Mum I'm sorry." I shouted over my shoulder. The man that had pulled me away from Mum gripped my arms tighter, and another man came over and started to tie my wrists in front of me. I could still hear Mum weeping behind me as she was cut down from the silver birch flagpole and retied at the wrists

137

too. Obeah walked towards the man holding me at the wrists.

"Give her to me." Obeah beckoned him to release me and the man pushed me away with vigour, my head jolted on my shoulders. It was an act of disdain I had never received before. Like he was pushing away a plate of stale food. Obeah grabbed me by my bound wrists and pulled me along as Thomas lead us through the clearing and into the forest that would lead us to the eastern beach – my favourite spot where the crows would squawk at the moon, and the nuthatches would sing to the squirrels. Now it would be tainted by Obeah's demise, or ours, and the odds seemed equally split.

15

Chapter 15

Some of the islanders disappeared at this point, but not all of them. Some were keen, hungry for the savagery to come. We entered the pathway into the forest, our world immediately darkened by the cover of the trees. Eventually Thomas's grandma spoke up from the back of the crowd.

"This is wrong Obeah." Her voice was frail and quiet, forcing everyone to turn toward her to listen close. He stopped dead and turned back to face the crowd, still holding tight to the ropes binding my hands. He lifted his chin so as to direct his voice over the heads of the islanders.

"You know better than to speak out against me Agnus." His voice reverberated out across the silence of the trees, not an animal sound, a crack of branches, or a gust of wind. The world appeared still apart from the heavy steel clouds that were forming above the bare treetops. It felt to me that the forest and the skies had been my protectors so far, I squeezed my eyes shut and tried to tune into my senses to calm myself.

"Your fall is coming. Let the girl and her mother go." Agnus, Thomas' grandma continued. Obeah gritted his teeth and turned to carry on walking.

"Go boy! Show me then." Obeah growled at Thomas like a snarling beast. Thomas started to walk faster his head turning from left to right, as if in the panic of it all he had forgotten where to take us. This was his route now, I had no idea where any of the traps were set. It hadn't occurred to us that we might be following one another's route. This was not part of the plan. Thomas lead us down a narrower path off to the right, I was trying to step carefully, I could feel myself bracing against every tree route, gasping at any dips in the ground. I was so afraid of falling into one of the traps. I never realised I was claustrophobic until I anticipated falling into one of those holes.

"Where are we going?" Obeah bellowed.

"We have to go this way. It's not much further I promise." Thomas reassured him weaving us through the trees, taking us on a less walked, less obvious path. Then, a loud crack echoed out into the air, followed by a heavy thump. I was jolted backward, as Obeah plummeted down into a hole set to capture him. He'd held my wrists so tightly the ropes had scratched and burned at my skin, but he did let go. He let go instead of pulling me down with him. Luca had been one of the soldiers hiding in the trees waiting for us. He had grabbed me at the precise moment I should have gone into the hole with Obeah.

"Come here." Luca said to me gently as he inspected my wrists. His long hair tied in a knot atop his head. He reached into his pocket and pulled out a small knife with a leather handle. He held both of my hands in one of his. My palms facing up, Luca sawed at the ropes with his knife, cutting into the space between my wrists. Luca was a giant of a man, broader even then Obeah, he could have grabbed that brute out of the hole, and beat him with his bare hands for his betrayal. But Luca was a gentle giant and he used his power only for good.

" Thank you, Luca." I rubbed my wrists. Obeah was hissing and growling from his hole. It was ten feet deep with nothing to grip onto. I peered over the edge to find him scratching and clawing at the dirt walls. Ten more soldiers, men and women of Nelawi emerged from the trees. Each stood by the remaining Islanders, each of them wore a leather belt that kept a dagger, and bow and arrow.

Though it was daytime the canopy of leafless branches kept the forest almost dark. Mum, still tied at the wrists, dropped to her knees and sobbed into the ground.

"It's over isn't it?" I asked looking to Luca for reassurance. He remained still and blank faced.

"It's really over." I said again feeling uneasy still. Luca looked around at his comrades who outnumbered the remaining seven islanders. They had come to witness the demise of two innocents; Mum and I. I ran to Thomas and hugged him. He stiffened in my embrace, but he did attempt a smile despite his discomfort. Luca went to Mum and helped her to her feet, freeing her bound wrists too.

"It's over." He soothed her.

"Fools!" Obeah shouted from his hole. He was shouting with all his might now desperate to be heard.

"Kunda still remains starved and entrapped. If she remains ignored. We will all die as she raises the waters and sends this earth quaking, and tsunamis to swallow us. *I* am the one who placates her." Even in check mate Obeah still grasped at his remaining power.

"You entrapped her. You have tricked and lied to her for years Obeah. *You* will set her free today." Luca bellowed walking over to Obeah's holding-hole. Luca stood there towering over his enemy. He pointed to a female soldier who stood to attention, he then pointed to Camille and Justin who were stood watching on. The soldier knew immediately what to do -drawing her bow and arrow she aimed her fire towards Camille and Justin.

"Obeah, you will free Kunda, or your only living family will be her next meal. I have them both here and under arrest." Luca warned.

"It's true cousin." Camille shouted out.

"Noooooo!" A male voice came from behind me. The man who had tied my hands. He ran past me to the hole and yanked at Luca's bow and arrow strapped across his back, kicking him in the back then - sending Luca tumbling down into the hole with Obeah. The crazed Islander, drew back the arrow in the stolen bow and lined it up. He let it loose at Mum.

"Owwwww!" She screamed out as the the arrow pierced deep into her right shoulder.

"Mum!" I ran to her. She looked down at the arrow and touched where it had pushed through her skin. Her eyes rolled backwards and she collapsed to the floor with a heavy thud. A twhip, thwip buzzed past my ear. And the man who had shot my mother was then himself, shot twice. He crumpled to the floor with two arrows in his back.

"Mum." I whimpered. And finally I broke. My heart shattered into a million pieces as I dropped to my knees and cried over my mother's lifeless body.

Thunder rumbled overhead, followed by a crack of lightning.

"It's already happening." Obeah yelled out from the hole. He began to laugh hysterically.

"*I* hold the power here. If I die we *all* die. He growled.

"Men split up. Three of you, surround the remaining islanders and the rest of you get me out of here." Luca called out. Following Luca's orders, three Nelawiti soldiers gathered around the onlooking islanders that remained including Camille and Justin who reluctantly complied. The rest of them looked empty and dumbfounded. They were herded into a group and surrounded by their shepherding soldiers who then froze, steadfast, awaiting instruction. Two soldiers came to Mum and I, while the remaining four went to surround the trap where Luca and Obeah had ended up.

"Throw me down some rope." Luca called out from the hole, and the soldier that had a leather knapsack strapped to his back reached over his shoulder, pulling out a huge length of rope and throwing it down to Luca. Another of those onlooking soldiers jumped in. Together Luca and the attending soldier tied Obeah up. The remaining soldiers winched Obeah out of the hole, followed quickly by Luca and his attending soldier. All bound up, Obeah began to chant and give his daily sermon anyway.

"*The Sky Ones* will save us." He cried out as he was pulled up over the top of the hole, Camille called out

"Obeah! My love, our Saviour."

"Shut up Camille." Obeah snapped. Justin looked more hurt than his mother at the reprimand. Thunder rumbled again, a murder of crows burst up and out of the treetops cawing loudly before disappearing into the clouds. Princess Nebatu and Francesca came walking slowly, majestically from the direction of the beach. Rain poured down from those lingering thunderclouds. Marmadukee, the eagle sat comfortably on the princess's leather gloved forearm. His blinders gone now, showing off the fire orange of his piercing eyes.

"My mum." I sobbed as the princess and Francesca arrived at the spot where I knelt over Mum. My knees frozen, my hands resting on Mum's cold cheeks.

"Soldiers we need to fix this." Princess Nebatu turned to make eye contact with each one of the fur and leather clad Nelawiti Army.

"Luca, Anwen's mother needs Kunda's venom to survive such a wound. The Goddess must be freed if we are to leave here alive." Her words were filled with faith and confidence. Obeah looked up from the floor where he lay bound, and still quietly chanting. He noticed Francesca then, and recognition brought his speech to a halt. He locked eyes with her.

"*You.*" Obeah seethed.

"You didn't think you'd get away with this forever, did you Obeah?" Francesca asked him with a soft smirk on her face. Obeah just stared at her, speechless.

"Real Sedna Islanders know that I am the one. I am the chosen one." Obeah roared out into the grey thundering skies. Francesca went on, addressing the princess now.

"We don't need him to free Kunda. I know where the caves are. Kunda will be set free today, and once she is Beacrow will learn of your deceit Obeah." She turned back to the man that had stolen her island.

"There will never be a place in paradise for you Obeah. To have played the Gods as you have. That will take a thousand lifetimes to repay." Francesca held his gaze as Obeah stared at her with contempt. The princess pressed on.

"You three take those islanders to the beach and hold them there." She instructed the men surrounding the herded islanders.

"Luca that man is our sacrifice." She pointed to the crazed man who shot Mum. He was still lying face down in the dirt with the two arrows in his back. I couldn't tell if he was breathing.

"Anwen's mother will need to be carried with us." She looked to the two soldiers stood by Mum and I. "Fetch the fishing nets. We can transport Miss Laura in those." The men ran in a rigid march back towards the beach where the Nelawi merchant vessel waited.

"Francesca, why don't you be the one to escort Obeah onto the boat?"

"Gladly." She replied.

"We can take that route to the caves thereafter." Francesca smiled. It was the smile of someone having served a very cold and satisfying revenge.

"The rest of you please follow Francesca, and ensure our prisoner remains compliant. Let's go." She beckoned to Luca, who quickly gathered the lump of injured man across his shoulders. The herd of people in their various states of demise began to filter towards the beach. I stood up as the soldiers returned with the fishing nets and carefully shifted Mum onto a large square of netting. They had weaved two large branches through the line and parallel to one another in order to create a make shift stretcher.

"Princess?" I asked, suddenly sheepish and afraid, and every bit an eleven year old girl needing her mum.

"Can I come to the caves with you all?" She wrapped her Eagle free arm around my shoulders, and I could smell the soothing scents of her leather skirts.

"Of course you can brave Anwen. Of course you can."

16

Chapter 16

Francesca led us to a series of caves that lived hidden in the Northwest cliff faces of the island. They would be impossible to see from ocean or land unless you knew where to look. The rocks and earth were granite black on this side of the island. The caves accessible by a man-made stairwell that had been carved and chipped into the rocks decades ago. Perhaps stairwell is too generous a description, but the carvers had left small but neat footholds. 33 to be exact. I counted as a way to calm my tangled, fear filled thoughts. The cave entrance was like going down into a rabbit's warren. The entrance was not much taller than me. Thomas, who had followed with us, (his grandma having ordered him to take care of me), had to duck low to enter the cave. It was the same for all the other adults in our party. Nine of us all in all. Our mission, to placate and free Kunda, who was apparently a giant serpent goddess, an angry and starving giant serpent goddess to be precise.

The floor of the cave was the ocean. It was as if we'd stepped inside a bowl. We had to find natural curves and ledges to stand up on. The princess, now eagle free having left Marmaduke on the beach, and Francesca, both held oil lanterns above their heads to light our way. There was enough of a ledge for all nine of us to stand carefully side by side. Luca holding the fallen Islander, arrows still protruding from his back, and the two soldiers holding Mum on her fishing net stretcher included. Our world was almost black now, with only the flickers of fire light reflecting on the inky black water below, and the light bouncing off the wet, craggy, oil slick walls of the cave. Our entrance took us to a central body of water. There were several other large tunnels heading deeper and deeper into the islands insides. Francesca began to chant, her voice echoing all around us, melodic and haunting. The surface of the water waved and then a splash. The lantern lights flickered.

"She's here throw him in Luca." Francesca ordered. My stomach churned and curdled. Mum began groaning as she regained consciousness. Relief washed through me. Then came a mighty rumble as a great slick black creature burst through the water's surface. The nine of us were stood 30 feet above the pool below. And this giant creature raised up to meet us at eye level. Her hiss and rattle echoed all around, disorientating us. Her emerald scales glistened like fire, and her giant eyes stopped on me. Obsidian, inside a ring of fire. She was every bit a snake. Her mouth opened, her fangs dripped with lava like venom. She roared out a strange shrieking sound that cut through me. I held my ears. Luca threw the dead man towards her. The splash of his body hitting the water pulled Kunda's attention from us. She threw her head sideways leaning away from us, and her body slammed back into the water. The splash soaked us all. The walls of the cave began to rumble, the beginning of an earthquake. Stray rocks fell from the ceiling above, crashing into the pool below. Kunda, the giant glowing sea serpent emerged again. Having eaten now, her body, a waterfall dripping and cascading back into the sea.

"Kunda, you have been wrongly imprisoned. You are right to be angry." Francesca spoke loudly. Her calm was mesmerising.

"You have been tricked and lied to. This is not the work of Beacrow, God of the skies. His job is to protect you and your lands. He has been lied to also." The serpent groaned and splashed back down below the surface once more. Francesca sang again. It was a language I had never heard. It was softer now, melodic, a beautiful lullaby. This time Kunder rose just enough to expose only the top of her head. Her eyes shining just above the water's surface. She was listening. Her hisses became a purr. She was soothed by the lullaby.

"To free you Kunda, we must fire our cannons into the walls that Obeah sealed. We need you to know you are not under attack. Please keep the island safe, control your wrath. Your torture is over." The shimmering serpent slithered down into the depths. The cave fell into silence. Lone droplets of water hit rock, echoing out.

"She is calm." Francesca whispered to us all. Thomas stood next to me and slipped his hand into mind. I squeezed, and he squeezed back, both of us reassuring the other. Francesca turned to me, and knelt to meet my height. Her tattoos shone in the shimmer of her lantern, her eyes dark and intense.

"The prayer to save your mother belongs to you. No wish or hope can carry as strongly as yours. You must speak to her now."

"I...I don't know what to say."

"Just say what's in your heart." Francesca urged me on. I cleared my throat and crouched low in an attempt to speak into the water.

"Great goddess Kunda. I... I...I've heard much about you. Lots of lies. I understand. I believe your power is meant for good... My mum she..." My words caught in my throat as a sob threatened to swallow me whole.

"My mum has a serious injury... She is a good person, a kind woman. I know her heart is pure. Please can you help us?" We all waited in the dark silence of the caves. The water still and glassy. And then. *Whoosh*. Kunda burst up out of the depths, her mouth wide open as she turned to face me baring her fangs. They dripped with a sapphire, gold liquid, pearlescent like the soil in Obeah's garden that day I took the strawberries.

"It's an offering Anwen, take this bucket." Luca offered from behind me. I held out the bucket for the sacred nectar. Francesca smiled brightly having seen this ritual before. I reached the bucket out towards the beautiful serpent Kunda. I reached as far as my arms could stretch, and then on my tiptoes. One drop. Two drops, then three. It was heavier than I had expected. As I pulled the bucket in towards me, I over corrected and slipped.

"Anwen!" I instinctively threw the bucket upward as I went down. Splash. Ice cold fear hit me. I kept going down, down, down, into the deep dark nothing of the water. Abyss.

Something came from underneath me. A floor beneath my feet, and I was rising up, holding my breath 87, 88, 89, 90. My head dizzy. Air. I gasped and choked and sipped at it. I was lifted upon the head of the great Goddess that had unknowingly created so much fear on Sedna Island. She tilted her nose and I slid from it on to the ledge where we'd all stood. I slumped to the ground. The soldiers that had been carrying Mum were already tending to her wound with the venom from the bucket, and then dousing it to her lips. The princess kneeled beside Mum, with her lantern held high to help the men see. She whispered prayers as the men worked. We had made peace between *The Sky Ones* and the Goddess of the sea.

Back in the light of day, the clouds had cleared and the sun shone upon Sedna Island. It was a warm contrast to the last few days. Princess Nebatu reunited with Marmaduke and her red kite, she set her men and women to raise the cannons. They sailed to the northwest corner of the island, and fired into the rock three, four, five times. Crows and seagulls circled above the ship as if watching over its work. We watched on from the eastern beach. With a quiet flip of an emerald gold body, Kunda was free. She returned to the open waters ready to roam the ocean once more. She was where she belonged. Birdsong returned to the skies of Sedna, as if in celebration.

"Where is my cousin?" Shouted Camille, still held within a group of captured islanders on the beach.

"He is held in custody on the ship where you will be soon." Answered the princess.

"He will have his one chance to speak up in court when we arrive back at Nelawi." She nodded in assurance of her honest intention to bring Obeah to justice. She held up her leather gloved hand towards the sky and her huge sea eagle, Marmaduke, set his claws out in front of him before landing upon her forearm with a lightness that seemed impossible for a creature of his stature.

"Good boy." The princess nuzzled her head into the bird's great chest. Marmaduke had another note rolled up and tied at his neck. The princess ignored it for now.

"Is she okay Luca?" The princess enquired. Luca was tending Mum, now laid out on the sand. I knelt at her side and held her cold hand in mine. She was wet with sea spray, and her dress was soaked and torn. She smelled of sweat and adventure. She smelled like my mum.

"She will be fine. Her wound has already begun to close up." He smiled. It was a kind smile, the smile of a gentle giant. Mum's eyes started to flicker before squinting open. The light of the sun blinding her. I shielded her eyes with my hands.

"Is it over? Are we safe?" Her words were a whisper and the lump in my throat dispersed into a short sob as I nodded at her, a small smile breaking through my tears. She lay her head back and closed her eyes, drinking in the warmth of the sunlight on her skin as she had often done back on Shelagh. I felt such a deep sense of relief. The princess gathered everyone together there on the beach. Even the outlanders had made their way timidly down from the hillside. She stood tall and proud, Marmaduke stood upon her shoulder now, her hair billowing gently behind her on the light breeze of the afternoon.

"People of Sedna Island. Whether you know it or not, you have all been living a lie, and you have all been living on stolen land. The true custodians were pushed out or killed, perhaps some of them were your parents, or your cousins. Maybe you remember, or perhaps you do not. It no longer matters, for justice has been done. With this in mind I have two choices for you all to consider." Marmaduke squawked in agreeance.

"For those of you determined to stand by Obeah, I admire your loyalty and I invite you to stand trial with him on his home soil back in Nelawi. You will be treated fairly upon my ship and kept in comfortable custody until the trial is done. For those wishing to remain here on the island you may do so on the agreement that you will follow the indigenous ways of this land, as offered by Francesca Mahala the only islander to make

151

it to land, and share the story Obeah's abuse with us." Of the 30 adults stood there, only a handful came to stand by Obeah. The rest chose to stay behind. Children began to appear from behind trees assured of their safety.

"Then it is done." The princess nodded and walked across to me.

"Come let us go find your friends." She wrapped her leather gloved hand around my shoulder. We walked up the beach through the east clearing for the last time.

Egret and her father decided to seek a new life in Nelawi. Her father had begun to remember things from before his time on the island and he felt certain that Egret's mother had come from there. He decided to hold an ocean burial for Egret's mum. He felt it would bring her spirit peace after so much suffering. After reuniting with his gran, Thomas decided he would also leave the island, his gran chose to stand trial with Obeah for treason.

"I did stand by and witness sacrifices that were not lawful." She admitted to all of us.

"I believed it was in the name of a God that demanded it, but I see now that I was wrong. It was all a lie."

"Was Mum one of them Gran?" Thomas asked her then. She was a tiny woman, frail looking and unable to stand up straight. But she had a strength to her, in the way she spoke and the way she looked people directly in the eyes.

"She was Thomas. I'm so sorry. She volunteered to go. No one could convince her otherwise, and I felt pride in her choice. I'm sorry." She bowed her head and allowed herself to be lead onto the boat by the Nelawi soldiers.

Francesca reappeared from the ship. She walked up the beach towards us all, looking every part the victorious warrior queen that she was. Her chest proud, shoulders relaxed. Not one fear took up space within her. She walked with a great sense of pride and ease now that she was home. She looked so happy to be back. She was home.

"Mum?" I spoke softly then, and her eyes blinked open.

"Yes sweetheart?" She smiled up at me, wincing a little in her pain.

"It's going to be okay Mum. Everything's going to be okay now."

The princess noticed then, that Marmaduke had an unread note tied at his neck. She unwound it and read silently whilst I helped Mum prop herself up onto her elbow. Everything was quiet for a moment. The islanders that were choosing to stay all sat scattered about the beach, still in their black clothes, looking forlorn, lost as if they had just woken from a horrible dream. The only sounds to fill the air were the squawks of seagulls, the sweet tweeting of birds high up in the treetops, the gentle lapping of winter waves against the shore and the crunching beneath Francesca's boots as she ran to meet two soldiers dragging a great heavy chest up the beach from the ship. I could probably have laid out inside it, it had great metal handles at each side. The chest was adorned with the most articulate carvings of trees, birds, beaches and vast great ships like the one we had arrived on the day before.

As Francesca reached the perfect spot between the people that would make up her new community, she flipped open the chest with one strong push. It was filled with fabrics of every colour of the rainbow; vivid linens and cotton's of deep reds, ocean blues, dusky purples and the yellow of the summer sun. She started to pull at them and flip them over her shoulders, releasing them out onto the sand with a vigour like a child digging into a fancy dress box. Once she had emptied the chest of what seemed like hundreds and hundreds of scarves, and lengths of fabric. She closed the lid and stood upon it ready to address her new people.

"This island is a land of sacred lifeforce. It's islanders were people that worshipped only the magic of nature. The miracle of life to which we owe our own survival. Our ability to eat, our ability to drink fresh water and sleep beneath the protection of the trees. The beauty of nature is all around us; a vivid colour scape. A cacophony of life blasting through our eyes in all its miraculous-ness. I urge you, islanders to relieve yourself of the darkness that has encroached upon you. Come-" She swept her arms out in a wide circle

"Pick the colour that calls you most, and be ready to begin a new, vivacious life of dedication only to the land and one's self. Let us be a collective of joy and happiness." She raised her fist into the air in victory. Those scattered around the beach watched on, not yet able to take that first step into a mysterious tomorrow. Princess Nabatu approached me then, looking suddenly more serious than triumphant. Her facial expression deadpan, unreadable.

"I think this is for you." She said as she handed me the note that she had pulled from the eagle's collar. It read:

> *We have located the sail boat known to belong to*
> *Cartographer Guy Macqueen.*
> *It is empty, but undamaged which suggests hope of life.*
> *Our search area has narrowed.*
> *We look forward to welcoming you home safe to*
> *Nelawi.*

"Mum look." I showed her the note.

"Oh Anwen. Your poor father. I'm so sorry. I never meant for any of this to happen. I just wanted us to be safe. I wanted you to have friends." She was gasping for breath at the long sentence. She lay back onto the sand and wrapped her uninjured arm around my neck pulling me down to her chest. And we lay there in that embrace for a long time.

"It's okay Mum. It's okay. There's still hope. They've found Shelagh, at least we can go home. We will get back to life at sea. There's still hope."

"I just wanted us to be safe." She whispered as she lay back again and drifted off into sleep.

"She's in shock." Princess Nebatu kneeled beside me. "We have to get her back to land, and to a hospital as soon as possible. Come." She took me by the hand.

"I will get Luca to carry her aboard and make her comfortable for the journey."

17

Chapter 17

A week later, Mum was still in hospital but recovering well. She had needed twenty stitches to her wound. But it wouldn't be much longer until we could set sail again on Shelagh. Our sailboat home had been returned to the docks of Nelawi. I visited her every day and began reading some of my old books. I had never got to the end of *Treasure Island,* and I had a new energy to do it, now that I was to become part of the search party looking for Dad. It seemed like anything sea based might offer me some newfound strength and inspiration for another adventure. I felt certain that Dad was out there somewhere. I had done all along. It felt good to have so many others believe it too. Especially Mum. When I wasn't visiting Shelagh, I would sit on wooden pallets at the busy docks of Nelawi's *Mortado.* This was a trading city. There was something exciting to see every day; exotic animals being exchanged for gold. There was an arctic fox that had managed to find its way onto a cargo ship in Nordaland. It had to be caught in the dock yard and returned. It was the most beautiful creature I'd ever seen. Its eyes the electric blue of the Nordic sky. The men who caught it did so kindly; bating the fox with with meat, and then looping it gently on a leash before crating her. They gave her a bowl full of whale meat and another filled with water for the journey.

On the first Sunday since arriving ashore at Nelawi, Mum and I had a visitor, an old friend I had always wanted to get to know better. It was Lord Parkinson of Betaland. The giant of a man with bright red hair to his elbows and a bright red beard which reached a point just above the belt of his kilt. He still wore that banjo across his body at all times, and he still preferred to answer serious questions in song form. He was a breath of fresh air after all those months of difficulty and loss. His songs were just as wise as I remembered, and as educational too. His favourite to perform remained *The Whale that got Away,* and my favourite to request was *Why do Humans like Animal Tusks?* Old classics from when Mum, Dad and I had first visited him on *Betaland*; a country filled with mountains and crystalline lakes.

"You must come again once we find your father. I can't help but think he is playing some wicked game of hide and seek with us." I smiled then as we sat side by side upon the giant wooden crates, watching the hustle and bustle of the docks. The smell of fish frying was the backdrop to all the other scents; sweat, animals and all things lost and rotting.

"I really hope that's true Lord Parkinson."

"You must start calling me by my first name, Merian. Your father did so much for the development of my country and its explorations of our surrounding islands. Our navigational skills have never been so sharp. I get to take the credit, but I am under no illusion that it was all the work of your father."

"Thank you Merian."

"I look forward to welcoming your mother and yourself to make plans at the castle when she is well enough. Until then." He stood and held out his hand to me. I shook it firmly, just like Dad had taught me. And he left, weaving his tall and towering stature between the crowds of busy folk working and trading. Chatter and bartering were the soundscape of this place, and I loved it.

Thomas and Egret enrolled in the local state school. They were so excited to come and tell me all about it when I was visiting Mum in hospital that day. They brought grapes and flowers, and stories of kind and funny teachers, of wonderful books and their first experience of poetry.

"It's like music but without instruments." Egret rambled on excitedly. I had never seen her so animated.

"If you like poetry, I have a book on the boat that you can borrow. I will bring it in tomorrow." I smiled "How is your dad?" I asked Egret then.

"He's settling into life without Mum. We've found a nice place to stay in town, and Thomas is giving him the chance to feel like he has a son, which is a great distraction." Egret smiled and nodded to Thomas, her legs swinging from the too-tall chair.

"That's good." I walked around Mum's bed to give Egret a big squeeze. I was doing that all the time, to everyone these days.

When it was just Mum and I left. I rested my head on her tummy, my first home as she liked to refer to it. She was becoming more herself, or the woman that I had always known anyway. The colour had come back to her cheeks, they were warm and rosy again. Her hair no longer tied back tight as Obeah had wanted. It was wavy and wild just how I liked it. How nature had intended it to be. She stroked my hair as we just lay there quietly in the open hospital ward surrounded by other patients sleeping or sharing visits with loved ones. Mum started to tell me a story, like she used to do

"I've learned something very special you know." She smiled at me, and I listened intently.

"Grownups try to fool themselves into thinking they can control tomorrow. They save money like pirates hoard treasure. They buy insurances to plan for the worst outcomes, to avoid anything scary or painful. But it's a false sense of control. It's a false way to feel safe and in command of tomorrow. I know that now. Because all it takes is one big storm or a bank folding. Insurances refuse to pay out, and our hearts aren't ready because we all tried way too hard to protect them. Hearts wrapped in cotton wool for far too long aren't kept at full strength. When I think back to our days on Shelagh, riding the waves and the wind... I can see now, that It's better for the soul to live exposed. Vulnerable to the unknown. Open to the mystery of tomorrow. Safe only in the knowledge that our hearts were designed to be strong enough to survive it."

"I think that's a wonderful lesson." I listened to my voice echo and reverberate through her belly as I spoke. It was like talking under water.

"I feel sure we'll find your dad you know. He's going to be furious with me."

"No, I think he'll just be pleased to see you." I smiled.

That night I stayed on Shelagh for the first time in nine long months. I was alone, but I did not feel afraid. Everyone down on the dock knew who I was and why I was there. I felt as though they were all looking out for me. I wandered the small rooms and corridors of my sailboat home. It all felt so familiar, yet strange and surreal. The green diamond carpets, the woodwork walls and cupboards. I went to my bedroom, and everything was just as we'd left it. My books, my teddies in their net hammock, my porthole looking out into forever. All I needed to feel whole again was Dad. As I sat down on my bed I noticed something. There was a sheet of paper taped to my bedside table. It was worn at the edges, and the handwriting was clearly Dad's. It was his favourite poem of all time, which meant of course that it was mine too

If you can keep your head when all about you
Are losing theirs and blaming it on you,
If you can trust yourself when all men doubt you,
But make allowance for their doubting too;
If you can wait and not be tired by waiting,
Or being lied about, don't deal in lies,
Or being hated, don't give way to hating,
And yet don't look too good, nor talk too wise:

If you can dream—and not make dreams your master;
If you can think—and not make thoughts your aim;
If you can meet with Triumph and Disaster
And treat those two impostors just the same;
If you can bear to hear the truth you've spoken
Twisted by knaves to make a trap for fools,
Or watch the things you gave your life to, broken,
And stoop and build 'em up with worn-out tools:

If you can make one heap of all your winnings
And risk it on one turn of pitch-and-toss,
And lose, and start again at your beginnings
And never breathe a word about your loss;
If you can force your heart and nerve and sinew

To serve your turn long after they are gone,
And so hold on when there is nothing in you
Except the Will which says to them: 'Hold on!'

If you can talk with crowds and keep your virtue,
Or walk with Kings—nor lose the common touch,
If neither foes nor loving friends can hurt you,
If all men count with you, but none too much;
If you can fill the unforgiving minute
With sixty seconds' worth of distance run,
Yours is the Earth and everything that's in it,
And—which is more—you'll be a Queen my love!

There was a lighthouse sketched at the bottom of the page, and I felt that there was a promise of return in there somewhere. The adventure of finding him was just around the corner.

As for Obeah, Camille and Justin? They stood trial in court as soon as we arrived back in Newali. They were afforded an independent judge and jury and still found unanimously guilty of treason for which the sentence would usually be death. But the people of Nelawi voted instead for life imprisonment for Camille and Obeah, and boarding school for Justin. Obeah's chants are often heard ringing out of the state prison, but they have no power here. For power is a thing that can only exist for as long as there is some belief in it. Power is a gift afforded by the believers; I've learned to be very careful about where I place my faith. I know for sure that the stars would never mistreat my trust, and so I place my faith in them forever and always. My guides into the unknown in this world and the next.

Printed in Great Britain
by Amazon